JACOB'S LADDER

JACOB'S LADDER

ALAN COLLINS

LODESTAR BOOKS   E. P. DUTTON   NEW YORK

Library of Congress Cataloging-in-Publication Data

Collins, Alan, date
  Jacob's ladder.
  Originally published: The boys from Bondi.
  "Lodestar books."
  Summary: The world of Jacob and his younger
brother Solly falls apart when they are orphaned and
pitched into a Sydney children's home, where other
refugee Jewish children are gathering as Hitler rises
to power in Europe.
  1. Jews—Australia—History—Juvenile fiction.
[1. Jews—Australia—History—Fiction. 2. Australia—
Fiction. 3. Orphans—Fiction. 4. Brothers—Fiction]
I. Title.
PZ7.C689Jac 1989 [Fic] 89-7647
ISBN 0-525-67272-9

First published in the United States 1989
by E. P. Dutton, a division of
Penguin Books USA Inc.

Originally published 1987 by the
University of Queensland Press,
Box 42, St. Lucia, Queensland, Australia,
under the title *The Boys from Bondi.*

Designer: Robin Malkin

Printed in the U.S.A.   First American Edition
10 9 8 7 6 5 4 3 2 1

for Rosaline and the boys

1

During the Depression years, we lived in what was formerly a very posh seaside guesthouse called the Balconies. It was sited on the highest point of land overlooking the grand sweep of Bondi Beach, so that any guest entitled to special treatment would be given the first-floor corner suite which had a verandah on two sides. From this vantage point, one could take in the entire panorama from the Bondi sewerage vent pipe above the north headland, to the sprawling graves of the cemetery that swept down to the very cliff edge of Bronte. Two massive gold-leafed glass doors with *B* on each guarded the entrance. You couldn't see much through the doors because of the intricate sandblasted waves and sea-gulls, but a little piece of the plush red hall carpet protruded beyond the doors giving a foretaste of the luxury that lay beyond. The first-floor verandahs covered the wide footpaths and were held up by elegant fluted iron stanchions, two of which still had iron rings bolted to them to tether horses.

When our family came to the Balconies in 1935, I was ten years old and knew nothing of its past sophistication. We arrived toward the end of summer—Father, stepmother Carmel, my brother, Solly, and me. The Chevrolet had snorted steam all the way on the short trip from Bellevue

Hill, quite rightly objecting to its reduced status. Portmanteaux were roped to its luggage carrier and to the footboards; the hood sides were tied back to cool the motor, giving the whole ensemble a most idiotic appearance. Even after Father had turned off the ignition, the engine continued to sputter on independently, like an aged person to whom no one listens.

My brother and I sat in the back, only our heads showing above the miscellany of clothing and household effects. Father's irritable call to get out and help was, under the circumstances, unheeded until Carmel, our stepmother, removed the overburden of rugs and carpets. Only then were her "two little mannikins" able to scramble out, smelling strongly of newly stirred dust. Father, fully laden, backed himself through the glass doors, beckoning us to follow him into that dim interior, the color of an Angelina plum. Carmel, her makeup sweat-ruined and with a temper to match, carried only her hatbox and a majolica vase through the doorway, letting it swing back on Solly, who took the full force of it on his nose. He dripped blood onto his shirt, then buried his face in the rolled-up curtains under his arm. I followed him closely, not wishing to meet the same fate. Once inside, I felt a chill of apprehension, a presentiment that this new era in my life was not going to be an enjoyable one.

My gloomy thoughts were halted by Father belligerently ringing a brass handbell and calling up the staircase, "Mrs. Stone, ah there, Mrs. Stone, it's me, Mr. Kaiser." The clapper of the bell had barely come to rest when two patent-leather-shod feet appeared descending the stairs. From my lowly line of sight, I watched as the rest of Mrs. Stone appeared, as though a shutter was being raised—first the shoes, then a purple crushed-velvet dress, a long glass necklace that swung to and fro on outsize pendulous breasts, two chins, two jowls, long thin nose with *pince-nez,* and a mass of tightly rolled hair that sat on her head like a horse's collar. She bared her teeth in a rictus smile and swept past Father to the brass jardinière which one of us had dislodged from its base. Only after it had been adjusted to her satisfaction did she acknowledge him.

In a voice that seemed to be forced out of her by bellows, she announced, "No need to ring, Mr. Kaiser, the dead at Bronte could have heard you." She restoked her lungs. "Your rooms are ready, what about the rent now, two pounds in advance, get your own firewood for the boiler, and five shillings if you want to put your car round the back."

Carmel started to say, "Did you get the lavatory fixed . . ." but Mrs. Stone, her lungs emptied, had already stormed upstairs. We were left an island of domestic detritus in a red-carpeted sea.

"The cholera on you," my father swore softly in Yiddish, then over his shoulder, "This way, Carmel, down the passage —Carmel, come away from the mirror for a minute. Watch the boys, don't knock anything over." He grabbed the two largest trunks and was swallowed up in the gloom of the dank, dark hallway. Carmel called after him, "Felix, if you're going to swear, do it in English; that Yiddish, it embarrasses me so."

He stopped in front of a paneled ochre-colored door, dropped his load, and inserted a huge key in the lock. It made a sound like a meat grinder on bones but functioned sufficiently for Father to kick the door open and lead the way into our new home. Bringing up the rear, I noticed the painted number 4 on the door and decided then and there I didn't like it at all. Nothing I saw as I entered caused me to weaken in this resolve. Smell—cold despite the dying days of summer; shadows—bizarre colors as a thin ray of sunlight

3

was bisected by the stained-glass fanlight above the only window, shrouded in full-length drapes. The beam caught the suspended dust particles before it hit a wall mirror and dissipated its feeble strength. Father killed the beam by pulling on the light cord, and a tulip-shaped candelabra high above us turned the dark into a pale yellow.

"The old devil's taken out the settee," Father yelled. "I know it was there when I came last week. Well, can you beat that?" He pointed to the wall and even in that weak light, I could see the light patch on the wallpaper.

Carmel said, "I begged you not to sell ours." Father rounded angrily on her, reminding her that her settee, together with every other stick of furniture, had gone to settle tradesmen's debts.

I was more interested in the totality of the so-called flat. The floor plan resembled those card houses we built where we constructed numerous cubiclelike boxes that had common walls on top of which we would endeavor to lay more cards to roof them over. But these cubicles had no roofs of their own—only the high plastered ceiling of the huge room we had entered. Little rooms with thin plywood doors seemed to open off in all directions. The partitioned walls reached up about seven feet, leaving a good eight feet above. We were, in fact, as Father explained later, living in the main dining room of the Balconies. The serving pantry had become our kitchen by closing it off from the main kitchen and installing a stove which had no vent, so that cooking fumes pervaded every corner of the flat. No matter what Carmel cooked, the smell would always be of something else, long gone.

By the evening, we had sorted ourselves out. Father and Carmel had the largest cubicle, Solly and I shared the smaller one, and the remaining box Father grandiloquently

4

called his office. From a mansion in Birriga Road, Bellevue Hill, to the dining room of the Balconies was a much greater distance than the hills that physically separated them.

Whoever called this period between wars a Depression was more than just economically correct. Our depression started within days of moving into the Balconies. Father's job as a commercial traveler in hotel supplies had ended months before, leaving him with a sample case of useless goods and a car that had left its vitality on the dusty roads of western New South Wales. It stood outside the Balconies for months with a FOR SALE sign on it until one day a farmer bought it, so he said, "to put in me hay shed and hitch the chaff cutter to it."

Uncle Siddy came round shortly after that. Flash Siddy —unscathed by the Depression except that the scale of his vaguely illicit, varied operations was scaled down, but never sufficiently to actually force him to offer himself for Susso, the government relief. How could he, while wearing a gold ring with a star-cut diamond sitting high in a claw that wore away the stitching in his trouser pocket?

"Felix, me son," he wagged his finger at Father, "here's what we are going to do, you and me. We're going on the road. Now sit down," he said as Father rose in anticipation of another of Siddy's law-bending schemes, "this is dead straight and might just get you all out of this dump."

What he proposed was this. All round Sydney and in the country towns, people were desperate for cash. If they only knew it, they had a fortune lying around in drawers. Old jewelry, gold—in rings, pocket watches, spectacle rims, mounted sovereigns, even picture frames and lockets. The two of them would go door to door and buy for cash, break it down, and sell it to the government assayer. And so they

5

did. When they worked the suburbs, they came back to our flat in the evening and emptied out the chamois bags on the kitchen table. Solly and I stood wide-eyed at their elbows as the two of them took the dropper from a tiny bottle of nitric acid, touched the gold, and watched to see what color stain it left. If it was a dull green, the gold content was over eighteen carat. Next, they took all that little mound of treasure and with a pair of pliers smashed up lockets to remove glass photograph covers; the floor would be strewn carelessly with pictures of soldiers, grandparents, and wisps of curly hair. After the rings and necklaces would come the watchcases. These heavy gold pocket watches with Waltham and Rolex movements were attacked ferociously, the intricate mechanisms they threw aside as if they were gutting rabbits. These were our part of the spoils. The beautiful balance and escapement wheels beat on like a heart outside a body.

Carmel was torn between desire and contempt for their enterprise. She would run her fingers through the sad remains of the lives of the poor, reading aloud the inscriptions on watchcases until Father snatched them away from her. Cameos in gold frames rested briefly on her neck only to join the twisted pile of gold before she could mouth a plea to save them for herself.

Once she said, "The Jews never seem to sell *their* family jewels, do they, Felix?"

Father dropped his magnifying glass in fright, but Uncle Siddy said, "They're not drinking away their savings either, Carmel, so shut up."

She swung round on him then and in a controlled fury spat out, "And I suppose they don't bet SP with you, Sid . . . much too clever by half, aren't they, eh?"

Standing quite close to him, I heard him swear in Yiddish, but the only word he allowed her to hear was the derogatory expression for a Gentile woman—*shiksa*. It's funny, I thought, out of all the lovely, gentle, warm, and comforting Yiddish words spoken to my brother and me, it was the hate words that remained longest in the memory.

For something over a year, Father and Uncle Sid worked the industrial suburbs of Sydney, but by then many others were also mining the same lode. Some were despicable cheats, telling the women at the door whose husbands were away seeking work in the country that what they had treasured as gold was, in fact, only rolled gold or even brass. In that year, we lived a little better than most.

Carmel's attitude to Solly and me changed in that time, too. We could do nothing right in her eyes. First she would nag us incessantly about our appearance, table manners, and laziness, perhaps with some justification. In moments of frustration, she mumbled about "caring for somebody else's bastards." Then we became pawns in a ferocious ongoing feud about money. Carmel started to buy furniture on time payment from a door-to-door salesman. The flat rapidly filled up with shiny veneered pieces until there was scarcely room to navigate a path. Father said very little except occasionally to criticize the quality and compare it with what we had in the Bellevue Hill home. Only when the food on the highly polished table became scarcer and almost uneatable did he stand up to Carmel. They blazed away at each other, he calling her a Paddington tart, she retorting that she was too young to be tied for the rest of her life to an old Yid.

At this time, I was, in a small way, an independent businessman myself. Uncle Siddy employed me to collect the SP —or Starting Price—bets. On Saturdays I sat bored through the Sabbath morning service at the synagogue but, straight after, changed my clothes and went on my rounds. With a billycan, I covered the surrounding Bondi streets collecting bets. A shilling here, two shillings there, the name of the horse and the gambler wrapped around the coins. Then back to Uncle Siddy at the rear of the barbershop, where he wrote them down in an exercise book. The race would then crackle over the wireless, and Siddy wrapped up the pitifully few payouts, and I went back on the round, kidding myself that the police knew nothing of this.

Uncle Siddy had tired of the gold-buying, and without his drive and impudence Father showed little enthusiasm for fronting the shriveled women, old before their time, who came to the door offering dead husbands' spectacles in return for a few more weeks of living. But Carmel held different views. "You don't need Sid, he's a shyster, Felix. Why don't you go to the country? You know the towns well." Oh yes, he knew them well enough, had traveled them for twenty years, was known as a good spender to all the publicans west of the Blue Mountains, drank with the police sergeants, and was guest at most of the service clubs. And now? Go back as a hawker—no better than some of those Jewish newcomers to Australia with their battered suitcases containing dress lengths and thin towels? Carmel wanted Father out of town, out of sight, and out of her bed as the squabbles through the cardboard walls clearly showed.

And the door-to-door salesman increased his calls to three times weekly.

He gave Solly and me threepence every time he called. A stocky, cocky, tight-suited, patent-leather-shoed mongrel with straight black hair parted dead-center, whose calling card was his payments book left on the hallstand. We took his threepence and went upstairs to our diversion. Mrs. Stone in the bath. Mrs. Stone seen naked in the full-length cheval mirror that reflected back in the hall mirror. Mrs. Stone, who never locked her door for fear of being found dead days later. The door to her suite stood open a few inches, and we flattened ourselves against the wall and watched enthralled as three afternoons a week at around four o'clock she filled the bathtub in her living room with buckets of hot water from the boiler in the backyard. Then she undressed in time to a Galli-Curci record on the gramophone. The ritual had to be completed before the record ended and the machine needed rewinding. Would she make it? Her gigantic whale-like body was finally unsheathed as the first trills sounded, then she lowered herself into the tub like a suet pudding, the water coming within inches of the tub top. We clutched our groins half in fear and half in an effort to subdue the strange tingling in the crutch.

Father came home from the country early one day. His clothes were torn, and he had a bandage around one hand. Angry, dispirited, and smelling strangely of liquor, he brushed aside our breathless questions meant in some way to stall him and ward off the inevitable. He pushed past us and slouched into the flat, straight into the bedroom. Within seconds he reappeared, his ruddy face as colorless and formless as Mrs. Stone's flaccid belly.

"The bitch, the whore, oh the slut . . ." Saliva trickled from the corner of his mouth. He turned to me as I tried to escape. "Look, look, my son, look at me hand. They put the dogs onto me in Mudgee, and I was only trying to make a living for us all—and she's doing that while me back's turned. Oh Alice, Alice, why did you have to die?" He collapsed like a winded colt and sobbed deep retching sobs into his dirty coat.

I backed away from this father, so different from the one I loved. At the door I hesitated a moment then fled down the passage. As I got to the hallstand, I saw the salesman's payments book. I grabbed it and ran into the street. This evidence of my father's misery I stuffed down the stormwater drain. The salesman came out seconds later, saw me, and growled, "Seen me order book, young shaver?" I shook my head. "If y' find it, Ikey, I'll give ya sixpence if y' bring it to me office." And he sauntered off as though he hadn't a care in the world.

The weeks that followed were unbearably tense. Father stayed in the flat, unshaven and wearing his dressing gown almost continuously. Until now, he had never hit my brother or me, but with every new outburst of fighting between him and Carmel, the predictable result was a vicious swipe at one or both of us. Sometimes he took his leather razor strop and flailed us about the legs. We took to staying out on the streets until exhaustion forced us to go home and try to get to bed unseen. We ate on the pay from Uncle Siddy's SP round. Carmel, on the other hand, became our protector, taunting Father with sneers of: "That's right, Felix, take it out on the kids, why doncha?" As long as the rent was paid, Mrs. Stone ignored the brawling of her tenants. After all, ours was not the only family to show the tenseness of the times by scrapping. The police had come to the Balconies before in response to a wife rushing into the street screaming she was being murdered.

Toward the end of that summer, a sort of peace came to our household. Exhaustion of invective and the approaching end of Father's savings forced him to take the last irrevocable step. He would go on Susso. Putting on his oldest clothes, he went down to the Council and applied for work or a handout. To his surprise, they offered him a pick and shovel and told him to join a gang building a walkway around the Bondi cliff tops. Two days a week. The job would last as long as the Council had funds to spin it out. He joined the other defeated men and put in his ten hours a day. The beatings and quarrels stopped. Father had other enemies. The men to whom laboring had been an accepted way of earning a living resented this soft-handed middle-aged Jew who had no right to be taking a job from their mates. With that fear of tomorrow that binds desperate men together, they conspired to make Father's work as hateful as possible. The gang foreman saw that he was positioned at the very edge of the cliff, picking away at the crumbling sandstone while the sea roared and crashed hundreds of feet below.

Father would come home, his face gray with fatigue and fright. His relations with Carmel were distant, even old-fashioned formal. If he spoke to her, it was in a stilted, clipped, economic tone, not wasting a word and dealing only in topics needed to keep the household functioning. Toward us, he spoke more and more as in the past, referring distressingly often to happier days when our mother, Alice, was alive. We hadn't the heart to tell Father that the door-to-door man had resumed his calls on those days when he was on relief work.

For nearly a year the job went on, Father getting more maudlin, given to sudden outbursts of tears and constantly looking at his broken fingernails and calloused hands. When the job inevitably ended, his breakdown was nearly complete. One day Solly and I followed him on one of his walks. He would shuffle down to the beach promenade, then turn up the cliff walk that he had helped build until he reached a rotunda of rock jutting out over the highest point of the cliff top. There he sat and stared out over the gray sea while the wind tried to whisk the old panama hat from his head. No matter what the weather, he followed the same course every day of the week, returning to the flat at sunset like the wheeling seabirds to their cliff-top nooks.

For my brother and me, had we known it, the end of a

chapter was about to be written. One day in midwinter of the next year, we came home from school, thinking only of the thick slice of bread and plum jam we would cut for ourselves. Pushing open the door of number 4 the Balconies, we entered to see it as bare as the day we moved in. The weak sun showed us the emptiness of our home. My brother scuffed the carpet with his toe where the indentations of the dining table showed freshly. I rushed from cubicle to cubicle to find the same vista of nothingness. Our clothes lay in a heap on the floor. In the kitchen, the loaf of bread was lying on the stove, an open tin of plum jam alongside it. But no knife, no plate. "No bloody nothin'," I said softly to myself. Solly called plaintively, "Carmel, Carmel, where are you?" His reedy voice bounced around the walls.

I took his hand, and we went outside the Balconies and sat on the step watching the sun go down and straining our eyes into its rays to be the first to catch sight of Father.

The sun finally sank reluctantly behind the buildings down the road, and we drew close together. Two men, big men with sharp blue eyes and dark hats, came up to us. One bent down and said to me, "What's your name, sonny?" I told him. "And is this your brother?" I nodded. He took a damp envelope out of another brown envelope and showed it to his mate.

The other squatted down beside me and said softly, "We're policemen, sonny, our car is just up the street a bit. We'd like you to come with us, okay?" He put his arm under mine, and the other man did the same to my brother. Together, unresisting, we shuffled to the car.

Solly shook himself free as they opened the car door and screamed, "Where's Daddy, we've got to wait for Daddy, he's coming up the hill soon." He sat down on the running board of the car, a compact little parcel of misery.

The two policemen talked softly a few feet off, then one said, "Sonny, is your mother's name Alice?"

My brother sprang up and shouted that her name was "Carmel, do you hear me, Carmel, Carmel, *CARMEL!*"

"Oh, damn," the policeman said to his mate, "what do we do now? Tell 'em, Bob, for Christ's sake, I want to get home for me tea."

"Look, sonny, there's been an accident. Your dad's fallen off the cliff and he's . . . he's . . . dead. But the part I can't figure out is that in this letter we found on him, he's put down his wife's name as *Alice.*"

2

When the police car drove away from the Balconies, my brother and I sat in the back, a slab-sided, blue-suited policeman between us. I could feel the hard shape of his truncheon against my leg, and once when he leaned forward was surprised to see that where his shirt gaped he wore no undershirt and his chest was a mass of dark curling hair. He took off his hat, and his head was almost bald. His mate steered the car in a stiff, formal regulation style so unlike the happy-go-lucky approach our father had used—weaving in and out of the traffic, waving to ladies, and generally behaving like a show-off of the thirties, which he was when the going was good before the Depression.

My brother was still whimpering, and once when his little body heaved with an enormous shudder of grief I tried to reach across the mountainous barrier of the policeman to comfort him. The policeman said, "He'll settle down soon, sonny, don't worry. What's his name?"

"Solly," I mumbled from the depth, "and he's nine. And I'm thirteen, and me name's—"

But the policeman interrupted me. "Jack, isn't it?"

I sat up a bit straighter and said defiantly, "No, it isn't. It's Jacob." I was astounded at what I had said because I really disliked being known as Jacob. I vowed to say no more. I looked out at the people on a passing tram with the superiority of a boy actually traveling in a police car.

The driver lit a cigarette, let it droop from the corner of his mouth, then half turned to his mate. "Can't remember ever having Yids in this situation before, Bob." He scratched his chin and went on, "excepting, that is, when Steeny the tailor was killed with his own shears."

Bob thumped him hard on the back with his fist. "Shut your mouth and just get us to the Shelter quick as you can." He dug his hand deep in his side pocket and pulled out a tobacco-flecked packet of peppermints and offered one to each of us. Solly took one, but I was frightened to open my mouth in case I either cried out loud or revealed a bit more about myself. With my eyes half-shut and peering through my lashes, I could think back on all that had happened, and at the same time keep a sneaky watch on our progress as the car growled up the Sydney hills and skeltered down the steep inclines toward the harbor front.

Except when a tram rattled past, it was quiet and dark in the car—just a glow of the driver's cigarette and the pretty dashboard lights. Solly had flopped back like a broken doll, his mouth open, his sobs escaping through his sleep. The car skirted the quay and turned up beside the south pylon of the Harbor Bridge. It nosed its way through the sandstone cuttings, where water dripped down the rock faces, until it halted in front of a building with a blue light outside and a brass plate that read, simply and chillingly, *Children's Shelter.*

The stilted official voice Bob had used when he ordered us into the car was now softened. Leaning across me to open the car door, he said, "Righto, Jack, here we are; you just go on in, and I'll wake whatsisname, Solly."

15

I shook myself alert and stepped into the road while Bob went to the other door and put his huge arms around my brother, depositing him gently on the pavement. I edged around to Solly and whispered to him, "Let's run, Solly, okay?" He felt for my hand, and together we took off down the hill toward the waterfront, the old cobblestones solid beneath our feet. Even as we ran like hares, I wondered why, with years of childhood training to be obedient to authority, we did not stop or hesitate for one second at Bob's bellows to "stop there, you little buggers!"

Three pennies jingled like alarm bells in my pocket as our downhill flight gathered momentum. I took them out and threw them behind me, catching a glimpse of Bob as he pounded after us. The oily harbor loomed up in front of us. The cold night air bit into my lungs, and as we got nearer the water I could smell the diesel fumes of the ferryboats. Solly no longer held my hand but ran pace for pace alongside me, his fine hair streaming out behind him; the tears had dried in streaks on his face, his eyes fairly danced, and I knew I loved him deeply.

As we reached the water's edge, a ferry sounded its horn. I heard the rattle of the gangplank being withdrawn. Now it was Solly who took the lead. Grabbing my hand, he dragged us to the ferryside. The ferryman put his arm across the gangplank, but we crashed through, sprawling full-length on the deck, watching with childish happiness the ever-widening gap as the boat with a great churning of water set us on a new course. The heavy figure of Bob with his hand raised in a suggestion of a half-wave was the last thing I saw before going below to stand shivering beside the beautiful, steaming brass boilers of the ferry, their massive shafts and rods pounding renewed life into Solly and me.

There was brass everywhere. It shone and distorted our

images, reflected back the dancing harbor lights, and vibrated minutely to the throb of the engines. Solly, watching me gaping, said, "Remember, Jack, how we used to look at ourselves in the backs of the watchcases?" I was jolted, not by the innocent remark in itself but by the realization that Solly at nine years was already reminiscing like a man halfway through his life. Tonight was surely a cutoff point for both of us; forever more, the demarcation would always be "the night we ran away." I nodded in reply, and a crazy elongated head in a flue pipe did likewise.

As we cleared the docks, a cool breeze blew away the diesel fumes, and to our right we could see the giant's teeth of Luna Park framed in the span of the Harbor Bridge. I stole a side look at Solly, half expecting him to exclaim ". . . remember when we . . ." But he said nothing, his chin was on his chest, and he swayed gently to the motion of the boat. I was angry at his silence. One of the few personal treasures we had managed to hide from Carmel's destructive swathe was a picture of Father and Mother photographed at Luna Park on a mock rear platform of the Melbourne Express. Solly was in her arms, I stood beside Father waving . . . not at a farewelling crowd, only a seedy photographer with his black hood and billycan of developer. The picture lay in a shoebox in our cubicle back at the Balconies. In my pocket, wrapped in tissue paper, was something else I knew to be important if only for the stealthy manner I came by it.

When we were about to leave our Bellevue Hill house, while Carmel scolded Solly endlessly, Father took me to the front door. From under his coat, he produced a screwdriver and very carefully prised off the little metal cylinder that was fixed to the top righthand corner of the doorframe.

"I know it says in the books that you shouldn't take a *mezuzah* down from the house, Jacob, but supposing a goy moved in, eh? What would he know of it? Probably think it was an ornament or some Jew junk."

He worked carefully until it came away, then showed it to me. It had always been too high up for me to see, and frankly I had been a bit frightened of it. Uncle Siddy was to blame for my fear. Smelling strongly of tobacco, he would grab me and lift me up to it, bellowing sarcastically, "Kiss the *mezuzah*, Jack, like a good little Jewish boy." And despite my struggles, on occasions my lips would be forced up against the little tube with its one opening like an eye through which I could see the Hebrew letter *shin*, the first letter of the unspeakable name of God. The little scroll contained a handwritten parchment with verses from the book of Deuteronomy.

Father gave me the *mezuzah* having first wrapped it reverently in the fine tissue paper he kept for gold. "For when you have your own home, Jacob." He had stuffed it quickly into my pocket as Carmel's voice drew near.

The ferry slid under the bridge, and I gripped Solly's shoulder so hard his head came up, his eyes widening in an effort to orientate himself.

"Where are we, Jack? Where are we going?" he asked softly.

"Stay here and I'll find out."

I surveyed the few passengers, trying to evaluate which face would give an answer and not be too inquisitive as to why two boys in thin clothing and sandshoes would be crossing the harbor late at night. There was some sort of voluntary segregation, the way the women all sat inside the saloon, their skirts tucked primly under their legs defying the playful tug of the breeze. As I made my way forward to the outer deck, some of them pursed their lips in disapproval. Staring stonily ahead, I went out onto the deck where pipes and cigarettes glowed.

The ferry rolled unexpectedly in the wash of a passing tug. Caught off-balance, I grabbed for the stanchion, missed, and fell heavily and untidily into a hard, dark serge shape that did not yield under me, not even when my flailing hands, seeking a grip, fastened onto cold, hard, shiny buttons. A pipe clattered to the deck, its glowing dottle flared for a moment then disappeared over the side. Its owner growled, threw me down, and bent to retrieve the pipe. When he straightened up, I saw the chrome numbers on his high stiff collar and the badge of the New South Wales Police on the cap beside him.

"You want to be a bit more careful, young fella-me-lad." In one smooth flowing action, he removed his cap from the seat and raised me up to sit beside him. "Going somewhere special . . . Ikey?" The saloon door opened, and in the sudden shaft of light I looked up into the pale blue eyes and fair, close-cropped hair. Ikey? In the velvety darkness was I identifiably an Ikey? Did I appear to the whole world like that coarse comedian, Mo, who did the Jews no favor during his thirty years on stage perpetuating an archetypal Jew, which in pre-war Australia was the yardstick by which all Jews would be measured? I rubbed my hand over my smooth face; there was not the slightest trace of the charcoal that was Mo's trademark. I licked my lips too, afraid that without my noticing, they had grown thick and slobbery like his. But no, I was still Jacob, thirteen years of age, brown hair, brown eyes, a bit on the thin side, and running away from the police.

The police! Here I was, bold as brass, sitting right alongside one who was smart enough to be able to identify me instantly as a Jewish kid, here on a ferry in the middle of Sydney Harbor in the winter of 1939. What hope would Solly and I have of escaping to God knows where if every policeman could take one look at us and say to himself, "There

19

goes that pair of Yid kids we're supposed to be on the look-out for."

The ferry threaded its way up Middle Harbor and started to edge into a landing. Some passengers headed for the gang-plank; the policeman never moved, his solid body transmitting warmth to me. As the boat neared the wharf, I could see the sign illuminated by the hazy blue light.

"I'm going to Gladesville to visit my aunty," I said and looked up into those clear blue eyes. It was not altogether a lie; Father had spoken in whispers about his Aunt Bertha, who shortly after her arrival in Sydney from London suffered a stroke and was admitted to the Gladesville Asylum. I was actually quite pleased to have a barmy aunt, and as he never took Solly or me to visit her, we could imagine what we liked about her. The policeman had relit his pipe. He demonstrated his great strength by lifting me down from the seat and giving me a gentle push.

"Well, go along then, young Ikey," he said. "Straight there, mind, and don't talk to strangers."

The ferry bumped the wharf, and I was thrown off-balance again but recovered quickly and shot down the stairs to find Solly where I had left him, with his back to the warm flue pipe.

"We're getting off here, Solly," I shouted to him above the roar of the engines as they went into a shuddering reverse thrust. I had to lever him away from his flue pipe. The engineer had given him a packet of potato chips, and he offered them to me. I brushed them aside and grabbed his hand, spilling the chips on the deck. Solly started to whine about it, but I lugged him down the gangplank and through the un-manned turnstile not knowing where I was going but suspecting that the young constable was hanging over the ferry's side watching us. The path rose steeply from the wharf; by

20

the time we reached the road, Solly and I were winded, the cold night air cutting into our lungs and robbing us of speech, which was probably all to the good, for neither of us had a clear thought in our heads.

I had lost all track of time—day, month, year. It seemed to me that there never had been a time when a clearly defined schedule of living existed, the sort of time that is marked by routine: You get up in the morning, wash, have breakfast, go to school, come home, go out to play until teatime, have an evening meal, chatter, then go to bed. Right now, as Solly and I huddled in a tram shelter, I would have given anything for one of Father's watches, to be able to hold it to my ear and listen to its reassuring tick. Like our family life, those watches were broken and discarded; Father was gone (I recoiled from believing he was dead); Carmel was gone too, but such was the depth of my misery at this moment, had she reappeared I might have run to her, not for comfort but as our last remaining link with the past.

A dog loped into the tramshed, sniffed at my feet, then put its head on Solly's lap. He pushed it away but it persisted, nuzzling into his crotch determinedly. Finally Solly stood up, and only then did I see that his thin pants were wet.

"You've wee'd yourself, Solly," I said critically.

He didn't reply but walked over to a rubbish bin, took a newspaper, returned to the seat, and spread it over his lap. He had seen the derelicts in the park covering themselves with newspaper. I too went to the bin and foraged among the rubbish until I had a pile of newspapers. With them spread over us, the dog at our feet, we fell asleep. How long I slept, I do not know; it must have been years when measured by my dream—a dream that had me locked in Mrs.

Stone's arms, her breast in my mouth. Warm milk flowed over, and I dreamed I grew to manhood. Then she changed into one of those half-naked women on the calendar in the barbershop. I came in a jerky stream that seemed unending.

When I woke, Solly was standing in front of me, his eyes wide with triumph.

"You've wee'd yourself too, Jack, so now you can't go crook at me anymore!"

I looked down at myself. The newspapers had blown away, leaving me exposed to a street where nothing stirred and the only sound was the approaching *clip-clop* of horse's hooves. Solly's pants had dried, leaving only a darker patina, but I bore the damp humiliation as the sky lightened with the dawn.

"Let's run and get dry like we do on the beach when our togs are wet," Solly urged, already jogging up and down on the spot. Together we set off down the road, sprinting strongly into the wind then gradually slowing down as our empty stomachs refused to pump any more energy into our legs. The red kerosene lantern swinging on the side of the milkcart brought us to a halt; the fat horse snorted steam as it pulled the cart at walking pace. We dropped behind it where the spigot stuck out. The milkman with his gallon can and quart jug could barely be seen as he weaved in and out of the front gates, silent in his sandshoes.

"Hold the horse's head," I said excitedly to Solly.

"No, you do it. I'm too small, I can't reach."

"Righto, I'll stop him, and you turn the tap and have a drink like we do under the garden tap. When it's your go, I'll leave the reins down so you can hold on."

I sidled up to the blinkered horse and took the slack reins. The horse tossed its head in disdain, almost lifting me off the ground as it maintained its steady gait.

"Hold him, can't you," Solly hissed from behind the cart. I moved around in front of the horse's head where its huge eyes stared at me impassively, its nose shoveling me forward in the chest as though I were weightless. We continued in this fashion for about twenty yards until the horse reached a patch of paspalum grass at the curb; there it dropped its head and munched contentedly. I joined Solly at the back of the cart where he was struggling with the spigot.

"Here, let me do it, you shrimp." I gave the handle a vigorous twist. The ice-cold milk came out in a gusher, splashing all over Solly's face, down his chest, and flowing into the gutter. He drew back, and we cupped our hands, gulping the milk like starving dogs. I could feel my stomach distending with the sudden intake; Solly had stopped and was squelching his toes in the milk banked up in the gutter.

"Jeez, Jack, turn it off before the milko comes," he shouted. I grabbed the handle and tried to stem the flow, which had now subsided to a thin trickle. Heave as I might, it would not budge; Solly added his diminutive strength, his small hands locked over mine. Suddenly, two mottled arms were around our necks, wrenching us away from the cart.

"Caught ya, y' thievin' little bastards! Think it's not hard enough makin' a livin' without puttin' up with this? It's off to the cops with you two—I've 'ad enough."

The milkman, chest heaving in his blue undershirt, released Solly who dropped to the roadway and vomited up the milk. With an arm still around my neck, he went up to the horse and unthreaded one of the reins. As though he had done it before, he tied the rein around my wrists then led me back to Solly and lashed the two of us together. Then with a free end around his own wrist, he sprang up on the cart and clicked his tongue at the horse, which resumed its amiable gait while the milko dextrously rolled a cigarette

23

one-handed, jerking us on the rein to trot alongside the cart. The miracle of that nightmarish progress of a half-mile or so to the police station was that nobody took any notice of us. Ignored by the milkman, the public, and the horse, we walked in tandem to its rhythmic gait, stopping only once when the milko got down from the cart to extinguish his red lantern. He took no more notice of us than if we had been a couple of cattle dogs trotting alongside. Solly's shirt smelled of vomit; his eyes were glazed, and he walked with a sullen springless step; there was obviously not an ounce of fight left in him. I couldn't have comforted him even if I wanted to; to my shame, I felt a mounting resentment that his shout had alarmed the milko and brought us both to our present predicament. The milkman flicked his cigarette butt away. With practiced ease, he swung himself down from the cart and went to the horse's head.

"Bloody soon have you two little buggers locked up," he called back at us. Grabbing the bridle, he urged the horse into a trot and ran alongside it. The slack reins tightened around our wrists, and we were jerked forward. At the end of the road where the tram tracks curved out of sight, I could see the blue light of a police station. I pointed to it and gasped hoarsely to Solly, "Nearly there, anything'd be better than this." Shafts of sunlight sneaked between the shops and houses, and the horse's damp flanks gave off a warm animal smell. Suddenly the cart stopped. We were outside the police station, a narrow-fronted Edwardian building of the style that would have done equally well for a bank or a church except for the ornate *GR* above the entrance.

The milkman came up to us and paused with his hands on his hips. For one moment our eyes met, and I thought he might let us go, then he shook his head as though fighting some kinder emotion. He untied the reins, linked his arms through ours, and propelled us up the steps into the police

24

station. There was a moment of comedy as the three of us tried to get through the doorway. Then the milkman released me and pushed me ahead. "In you go, Ikey," he growled. The hair rose on the nape of my neck. "Lousy milk waterer," I shouted over my shoulder, but all I got for my abuse was a stinging clout over the ear and a roar of laughter from somewhere ahead of me. The milkman pushed us up to the counter. I could see nothing but an expanse of cotton undershirt and heavy braces; Solly's eyes were dead level with the cedar edge, gouged by time like an old school desk.

"These bloody kids was thievin' me milk, sarge. Bold as y' like they was, an' then they left the bloody tap run, and all me milk ran out." He bent down and hoisted Solly up on the counter. "They'll put the pair of yers into the bad boys' home, that's what they'll do—won't yer, sarge?"

The sergeant hooked his fingers into his braces and rocked back on his heels. He was the biggest man I had ever seen; his thinning red hair and mottled face sat atop a girth as generous as the milkman's horse. Instinctively, I felt I had nothing to fear from this avuncular giant who now looked past us with a quizzical smile at the excitable milko.

"Do you want to make out a charge, Perce?" he asked in a half-serious tone. "And while you're at it, we can talk about the SP you collect and Mrs. Moloney's complaint of watery milk." He pressed a bell on the counter, and a young constable appeared.

"Stan, get these kids a cuppa tea, will you?" He turned to the milkman. "Now, Perce, where were we?" But Perce was gone; through the open door, we could hear him geeing up the horse, the rattle of his cans echoing down the empty street.

Stan came back with two thick cups with *GR* in red on the side. The scalding sweet black tea was thrust into our cold hands. "Sorry we haven't any milk, boys," he said, then laughed uproariously. "I reckon you've had enough of that stuff anyway!"

The sergeant sat down at his paper-laden desk, taking no notice of us as we slurped at the hot tea; I watched his stubby fingers turn over the pages of a leatherbound book. He took a blotter and used it to run down the entries—down one column, up the next, turn over the page, down again —then stop. He held the blotter at the entry and looked up at us, then down again.

"Jacob Kaiser, aged thirteen, and Solomon Kaiser, aged nine, of the Balconies, Beach Road, Bondi." He closed the book softly and came over to us.

"That's you two rips, isn't it?" I liked the sound of our full names; except from schoolteachers who made stage-Yid jokes about them, I had never heard anyone pronounce them with dignity before. Solly looked to me for objections, but I had none; he got down from the counter and stood proudly beside me.

The sergeant indicated two chairs. "Sit down, boys." He delved into a desk drawer and came out with a packet of sandwiches. Opening them, he looked at the fillings, shook his head, and said quite sincerely, "Sorry, can't offer you these, the missus put ham in 'em." He turned the glowing radiator toward us, leaned back in his swivel chair, and said, "Bit thin, aren't you? I always thought Jewish kids were fat. Blimey, when I was stationed at Waverley I used to see them going to their church on Saturday, dressed up to the nines, plump as frankfurts. Just like the dago kids."

Solly had been watching him intently; I felt sure that had the policeman moved suddenly, Solly would have been out of his chair and on the run again. There was silence except for the big clock ticking away, high up on the wall. It was a little after seven—about twelve hours since we fled from the

Children's Shelter: for Solly and me, an expansion of time that aged us with experience and bewilderment.

I said: "How do you know who we are? Have you got tracker dogs or something—like Rin Tin Tin?"

"Look, come over here and I'll show you." Behind a tall bookcase, there was a radio receiver. The sergeant flipped a switch and beckoned to Solly, who came forward nervously. "Put those headphones on, young'un, and listen." Solly did so; they fell over his ears but not before his eyes lit up in wonderment.

"They're talking, Jack," he said in awe, "all about cars and things." There was a high-pitched oscillation, and Solly ripped the headphones off.

The sergeant switched the receiver off and said, "We got the message from the Rocks Police that two boys had given them the slip and jumped on the Gladesville ferry. We had nobody free to look for you last night, but I intended to look myself this morning." His eyes twinkled. "Fancy robbing poor old Perce of his milk—you could get twenty years for that!"

Stan came back into the room and looked at the sergeant expectantly. The sergeant shifted his bulk in the creaking chair and mumbled behind his hand, "Let's not rush this, Stan. I'd like to ask the kids a few questions. Bring us some more tea and find some cookies." When Stan had gone, he leaned forward and said: "I should take you back to the Shelter but, Christ, you'd get into more strife. Now, how about telling me what's going on, eh?"

The awakening day, the warming tea, the sound of trams rattling by outside, and the reassuring bulk of the policeman without his jacket all conspired to relax me as I told him of the events that had brought us to this point. At only two stages in my recital did he show any reaction. When I told him of the salesman's frequent visits to the Balconies, he murmured, "the bastard"; the death of our father brought out a further "poor bastard," and he shook his head. I described Carmel in hateful terms, refusing to call her mother, only stepmother. Solly's body stiffened and he opened his mouth, but thought better of it and said nothing. Stan came back with more tea and a plate of arrowroot biscuits.

"Gawd, Stan, is that the best you could do? Never mind, dig in, kids. Now, tell us about your Uncle Siddy. Is he your dad's brother?"

Solly said importantly, "Uncle Siddy wears a diamond ring and he's got a car, a big one, just like a police car!"

"Go on," the sergeant said admiringly, "y' don't say— and has he got a telephone too? Would you like to ring him?"

Solly looked at me for guidance. "Has he, Jack? Has he got a telephone?"

I shook my head. "He's in the country somewhere," I told the sergeant. "He—he buys and sells things."

The thinnest edge of authority tinged the sergeant's next question. "Would you sooner we contacted him or maybe Mrs. Kaiser—or shall I call her Carmel?"

Had I been older and wiser, I would have recognized the policeman's ploy of offering two unattractive choices, knowing I must choose the lesser of two supposed evils. As it happened, the reply he got was less than satisfactory. Solly was in no doubt and plumped for Carmel while I said Uncle Siddy in a take-it-or-leave-it voice. By the time they found him, I thought, anything could happen—we might even escape again, go up the bush, live like outback cattle drovers, fish in the Murray, and sleep under a wagon with a cattle dog to guard us. . . .

The telephone bell cut into my daydream.

"Yeah, yeah, they're here, Bob, caught steal—found 'em asleep in a tramshed. Bloody shame about the old man . . ." There was a pause while the sergeant listened. His big hands clenched into fists, the veins rose up like knotted string. "I don't care about the coroner, you're not taking these two to the morgue and that's flat! You get off your arse and find a bloke called Sidney Kaiser, the old man's brother. Let him go, not these poor kids." He slammed the phone down, and seconds later it rang again. "Oh, it's you again, Bob. You've got who there? Mrs. Pearlman? From the what? Hang on, there's a tram going by—wait, I'll write it down, now slowly: Mrs. Pearlman from the Hebrew Philanthropic Society, and she wants to take charge of the kids—have I got it right?" The sergeant listened carefully for a bit longer, scribbled on his pad, then hung up the phone. "Did you hear that, Jacob?" he asked. Not waiting for a reply he stood up, signifying that as far as he was concerned, this was the end of the affair.

"I'm to put you two in a taxi and send you to Mrs. Pearlman at"—he referred to his notes—"the Maccabean Hall in Darlinghurst Road. Now, the big question is: Can I trust you two young rips to behave yourselves?"

I looked at Solly; to my amazement, he was sound asleep, his head sunk on his chest, his breathing soft and regular. I stood up without disturbing him and said quietly to the sergeant, "Yes, you can," in my best adult voice. He put out his big hand and I shook it.

"Look, Jacob," he confided, "I know the Yids—er, Jewish people—have a good name for looking after their own. I'm sure everything will be okay. I remember when Steeny Isaacs was stabbed in his shop in Paddington, how all the family came round, even a funny little rabbi fella. In no time at all, that family was back on its feet. You've got to respect 'em for it. One word of advice though, Jacob, stick with the little bloke—he's going to need you." He called out to Stan to get a taxi. I sat down again, and the sergeant shuffled his papers officiously until the cabby slouched into the police station. The sergeant took him aside, there was a whispered conversation, then the sergeant pressed a pound note into his hand.

I woke Solly gently, took his hand, and led him, still half-asleep, into the cab. I sat in the back with my arm around Solly; the ticking of the meter lulled me to sleep too, and I knew no more until the driver was standing by the open door. "Here you are, Ikey, at the Jews' Hall. Ha, ha, lucky I got paid first, eh!" He hauled us out and left us on the pavement.

3

Solly leaned against a lamppost and asked drowsily, "Do we have to run again, Jack?"

I shook my head, took his hand, and led him up the long flight of stone steps into the foyer of the building. There were hundreds of names on an honor board and a marble soldier's helmet below it. In the dim light I started to read them. Suddenly I stopped and grabbed Solly excitedly. "Look up there, Solly!" I shouted exultantly. "Sidney Kaiser, it says —that must be Uncle Siddy—he was in the war and there's his name!"

Solly said, "That's nice, Jack," yawned, and sat down immediately on the marble helmet.

Discovering Uncle Siddy's name on the honor board had a strange effect on me; I felt it somehow gave our family real substance, proving that I actually existed. If I ever doubted there had been a mother named Alice, a father named Felix, and that we once led a loving life in Bellevue Hill, I had only to return here and look at that name perpetuated in gilt.

Suddenly a woman appeared silently at my side. She followed my staring eyes then said in a metallic voice, "You'll get a stiff neck, Jacob."

I said proudly: "That's my Uncle Siddy's name up there."

She raised her arm and pointed to another column of gilt names with stars behind them. "See there—Pearlman, Norman? That was my husband. Now, you two are Jacob and Solly Kaiser, aren't you?"

It seemed to me that the whole world knew who we were; what was there to be gained anymore by running? From now on, we would be identifiable to whoever wanted to find us. I wanted desperately to be anonymous and at the same time to be able to come here and look at this unalterable evidence of my existence. I could see we were in for another interview. I felt wary, even truculent toward this slightly built woman in her self-effacing, subdued print dress, who nevertheless had an unarguable air of authority. I stood almost to her shoulder, could see the tendrils of hair that escaped a tidy coiffure, enjoy—in an indefinable way—the pressure of her breast against my arm. Swallowing hard, I tried to subdue the pleasure it gave and drew away from her. In a gruff voice, I ordered Solly not to sit on the helmet. He rose languidly and asserted his presence by declaring that: "It was *my* Unce Siddy too."

Mrs. Pearlman said: "Come into my office, boys. Would you like a nice hot cup of tea?" Solly and I looked at each other, our cheeks puckered, and we burst into laughter— pent-up, hysterical, frightened cackle that echoed around the marble foyer. Mrs. Pearlman made no effort to stop us; she waited unmoved until it ceased then led us, unresisting, into her office, a small windowless cubicle whose chief adornment was an almost life-size photograph of a soldier. She left us alone, with him to guard us, while she fetched the tea.

"Now," she said as she handed us tea in pretty floral cups, "I suppose you are wondering how I came to know about you. Do you remember Mrs. Stone, the landlady at the Balconies? Such a sensible woman, I wish there were more like her who knew the right thing to do in such circumstances."

32

She paused and sipped her tea. "Mrs. Stone has told me all about you and about your poor unfortunate father." Her eyes rose to the picture on the wall, and she murmured softly, "So many good men die." As yet I did not understand her gratitude to Mrs. Stone; while she talked of a home for Jewish children where they would be cared for and brought up to respect their ancient faith and how we must not be allowed to become wards of the state, I hardly listened. My thoughts were of Mrs. Stone in the bath and if she had ever discovered our peeping and even told Mrs. Pearlman.

There were no questions from Mrs. Pearlman; she knew more about Solly and me than we knew ourselves. We sat quietly like a pair of garden gnomes that would soon be shifted without query from one place to another. We took no interest in what she was saying, so it came as a shock to find that, like a tourist guide who reaches the end of his pitch, she had risen from behind her desk and was already leading us out into the wintry sunshine.

Mrs. Pearlman shepherded us across the road to a parked car. She sat us in the back on a high seat open to the air, leaned through the window, and said: "We've a long trip, Jacob—we are going to Lindfield, across the Bridge. Have you ever been across the Bridge in a motorcar before?" and without waiting for an answer, pulled on her gloves and got into the driving seat. I was fast becoming something of an expert on car-driving techniques. Mrs. Pearlman, sitting up straight with her gloved hands holding the wheel as though it might answer her back, steered the car belligerently into the flow of traffic. Not for her the indolence of our father or the arrogance of the policeman or the irritability of the taxi driver: The car was her inferior, it would do as it was told —or else. Solly and I were as detached from her as if we were passengers on a train and she the driver far removed from us.

Once across the Harbor Bridge, the traffic thinned, and she dropped her shoulders slightly and wound down the window. The cold air ripped into our thin clothing. We jammed our knees together and held our arms tightly across our chests, jaws clamped tight to stop our teeth chattering. Where there were tramlines, Mrs. Pearlman followed them exactly as though they were magnets drawing her forward; when they went their own way, she lined up the car wheels with the yellow line down the center of the road and never deviated from it. Suburb after suburb flashed by; we had left the densely populated areas behind, and the white Pacific Highway was marked on either side by large stone bungalows with front lawns as big as parks. Some had white storks poised over giant clamshells.

Suddenly we were thrown violently to the right as, without warning, Mrs. Pearlman swung the car off the highway and down a steep, rutted road with trees arched across it. The notes of bellbirds came clearly over the racing engine. The car plunged on like stormwater down a drain until with a frightful grinding of gears it paused momentarily before turning into a driveway that wound between tortured gums. Low branches lashed the side of the car as Mrs. Pearlman drove on the high sides of ruts to avoid the water-filled depressions. Then we heard the purr of asphalt under the wheels, and the car halted in a green clearing flanked on two sides by a stark, low building of pink bricks.

With one action, Mrs. Pearlman was sounding the horn and opening our door. My first sensation was one of pleasure at the warmth of the morning. Without the rushing wind in the car, the sun curled around my shoulders, and I could feel my taut frame respond, unwinding like a cat by a fireside. I turned my face to the sun, smiling stupidly back at it as though it were a friend I had not seen for a very long time.

"Isn't it beaut," I whispered to Solly.

"It's a very big house," he replied.

"The sun, Solly, the lovely warm sun, ah, it's all over me." He stood beside me, his little chin tilted. Unconsciously my arm went around his shoulder, and there we stood oblivious of everything except that marvelous pervading warmth. As though from afar, I heard the car horn sound again, heard the crunch of feet on gravel, the low murmur of voices, felt us being propelled gently forward up some steps, and only when the eaves of the building cut off the sun's rays did I come back to earth. The cold that was only a shadow returned and enveloped us. It had a voice that was saying our names and asking us questions, hands were patting us, poking us, stroking us, but I had withdrawn inside my head where the sun still shone, and nobody could ever take it away from me.

Inside the building there was a smell of newness everywhere. It came off the painted walls, the polished floors, even the chairs on which we sat, across from a man and woman whose faces glowed pink, scrubbed and shiny. Above their heads was yet another of those honor boards, which I scanned while the couple conversed with Mrs. Pearlman. Perhaps Uncle Siddy's name was up there as well. It was divided into a number of columns with headings that read: *President* (only one name there); *Life Governors* (six names); *Life Members* (too many to count); and *Committee* (six names). Uncle Siddy was not there. I nudged Solly to look. He read the names slowly, his mouth working as he did so; then in his high clear voice, which bounced around the room, he said: "Uncle Siddy's not there, Jack."

The three stopped their conversation, and the man spoke in a strange accent. "Not where—who is not there?" Mrs. Pearlman tut-tutted admonishingly at Solly and explained.

"Ah, Mr. Goetz, little Solly has seen the Memorial Board at

the Hall with his Uncle Sidney's name on it. He thought—"
"—our peoples here are from the war, yes?" he broke in.
"No, younger man, these peoples are our—how do you say it, Mrs. Pearlman?"
"Our benefactors, Mr. Goetz. Yes, that would be right."
Solly burst out laughing. "Is your name really Mr. Goats?" he asked and put his fingers up to his head like a goat's horns. The man stood up and gripped the edge of the desk, but the woman tugged at his coat then spoke rapidly to him in a foreign language. He controlled himself then smiled hugely.

"I am not a goat, younger man, and you, you are not the Kaiser either. So, let us be friends, yes, and you call me Mr. Goetz, like in shirts, and this lady is Mrs. Goetz, also like in shirts." He leaned across the desk and stuck out his hand. Mrs. Pearlman nodded to us, and we went to him and solemnly shook hands.

His wife beamed approvingly then clapped her hands and said, "Now, shall we have some tea?"

Mrs. Pearlman saved the moment for us by cutting in quickly, "I think it is time these two gentlemen had a bath and some wholesome food, Mrs. Goetz. God knows when they ate last."

To this day I have the strongest recollection of Mrs. Goetz. It was her sheer size, well over six feet tall, her gigantic bosom, muscular neck, and perfectly oval head with tight black hair that crowned a face with skin drawn tight over a bone structure that would have done credit to a circus strongman. As I walked behind her, the calf muscles flexed through her stockings, driving each foot forward like pistons on a steam engine. Mingling with the smell of newness was her own personal odor of strong carbolic soap and the creak of her heavily starched uniform. Without realizing it, Solly and I fell into a marching step behind her, covering miles of polished floorboards, through vast halls until we came to the kitchen, which was bigger than our entire Bondi flat. She marched across the tiles, her heels ringing out her advance. A plump little woman sprang to attention beside a bubbling tureen, lifted the lid, and silently handed her a ladle. Mrs. Goetz dipped it in, blew on its contents noisily then beckoned me to taste.

"*Ess*, young man, *komm*, eat the soup."

I sucked clumsily from the hot ladle with Solly watching me apprehensively. It was rich and brown with the tiniest globules of fat dancing on it like gold dust. No words were necessary for Solly to see that it was good; he reached up and took the ladle, emptying it half down his shirtfront.

"*Ach* so, young men, please sit here, and cook will give you soup and bread but no butter, eh? Here everything is kosher—you know what that means?" I didn't know that it applied to food. The word had a different connotation when mouthed frequently by Uncle Siddy. Deals were kosher, the man who bought the scrap gold was kosher, the woman he was currently living with was not kosher. I never realized that its true meaning applied to the strict observance of Jewish dietary laws. Mrs. Goetz was merely telling us that here one did not eat dairy products with meat. There was a lot to learn.

Mrs. Goetz sat facing us at the kitchen table, watching with obvious enjoyment as we ate. Solly burped. She wagged a finger at him, but her eyes were smiling. When we had finished, she stood up and issued her commands—baths, wash the hair, cut the fingernails, clean clothes, and then, "You will be ready for when the other children come home from school, yes?"

Other children? What other children? Where did they

come from? How did they get here? Mrs. Goetz's matter-of-fact statement sent my mind reeling. It simply had not occurred to me that there would be other children here; in my own tight little world, there existed only Solly and me, a past that would not go away, and a future that I had never bothered to think about. Now as we marched behind Mrs. Goetz's broad back, I saw with confused feelings the straight rows of dining tables each with its own little vase of artificial flowers. A sharp left turn and we entered a long dormitory of eight beds with bright blue covers; our little column continued down the center of the dormitory, through swinging doors and into a bathroom of blinding whiteness.

"Here is water, here is soap, here is towels and"—she reached into her uniform pocket and brought out a brown bottle—"you should put this on your head but be careful, not in the eyes, yes?" She took the top from the bottle, and the smell of carbolic filled the room. "Soon I shall return with the new clothes." The swinging doors closed behind her, and we were alone.

We turned on the water and stood gazing as it slowly filled the baths. "Couldn't we just pretend, Jack?" Solly said. "What if the other kids come in, what if a girl comes in and sees you with hair round your dicky?"

"There aren't any girls here, stupid, this is the bad boys' home, like the milko said," I replied halfheartedly.

"Are we bad boys, Jack?"

"I suppose so, else we wouldn't be here, would we?"

"I liked the soup."

"What do y'reckon about Mr. Goats, Solly? I thought he was gonna give you a clip in the ear."

"You'd have belted him, wouldn't you, Jack?"

"Too right and I'd 've told Uncle Siddy."

We watched the mounting bathwater, undecided. Finally,

with Solly watching me for a lead, I turned the taps off. Silently we undressed and stepped into the baths. It was glorious. My skin tingled, the fine hairs on my arms lay in beautiful patterns, and the heat was a full summer sun nurturing me like a mother.

Solly was splashing around like an otter, water slopping over the edge of the bath. Neither of us had picked up the soap, but the water was already murky with a gray sludge tidemark. Far off, I thought I heard something that alarmed me.

"Be quiet a minute, Solly. I thought I heard voices." We both lay still in the water. There was no mistaking it; through the window slats, I could hear girlish laughter, then a boy's voice calling, "I'll catch you later, Ruti."

"Bloody girls, Solly. Oh Christ, they might come in here. Get out, quick. Jesus, they might even be bad girls."

I pulled the plug and jumped out. The water made a rude gurgling sound, mocking our fears. The swinging doors opened, and Mrs. Goetz stood there.

"So soon finished, young man? Okay, get dry and come with me."

I wrapped a towel around me and stood there manfully. "Are there girls here, Mrs. Goetz—in this place?"

"Of course, Mister Jacob, there are five. There's little Anna and big Renate, they are sisters. And then there is Goldie and Ruti and Erica. But don't you worry, boys too we have for you to play with. Come, come, you will soon meet them." She wrapped a towel tightly around Solly and picked him up effortlessly. I followed her through the dormitory to a room that was really a gigantic cupboard.

From floor to ceiling, it was stacked with clothes—on hangers, on shelves, in drawers—meticulously categorized for size, for winter, for summer, for boys and girls. Yet unlike the rest of the home with its raw smell of newness, the windowless clothes room reeked of a potent aroma of moth-balls and dry-cleaning spirit. Mrs. Goetz stood back and sur-veyed us critically, then paraded back and forth along the shelves, selecting items which she placed in two neat piles on the table.

As I stood there in the damp towel, my body cooling rap-idly, I could hear laughter and shouts coming from the dor-mitory. Mrs. Goetz grinned at us and said, "Quick now, younger men, *du* must get dressed." And she added impishly, "Before the girls *komm,* ya!"

She pushed my pile of clothes toward me: undershirt, shirt, underpants, short trousers, and a sweater with school color bands on it. All the outerwear had woven, scripted name tags sewn into them, and each item had a different name. I looked at them in horror and distaste. They were the clothes of dead children, I told myself. After they were put in the ground, someone had gathered the clothes up and brought them here. They smelled of hospitals. The owners would appear in the night and demand their clothes back. They might even kill me for wearing them! I shivered uncon-trollably. Then as Mrs. Goetz turned to me and saw that I had made no move to dress, I swept the pile to the floor and burst out crying.

Solly, who was already half-dressed, stared at me uncom-prehendingly; he sat on the edge of the table where Mrs. Goetz had been trying shoes on him.

"Don't wear them, Solly," I cried, "they're dead boys' shoes."

He looked down at his feet. "They feel nice, Jack. Can I keep them, Mrs. Goetz?"

Mrs. Goetz calmly picked up the fallen clothing as if noth-ing had happened, waited until my sobs had subsided, then crooned, half to herself, "Jacob, Jacob, it is good that you cry; such times you have had need to cry. But Jacob, my young man, you are wrong—these clothes are from our committee. How do you say it? The kind people have children who have grown too large for their clothes, so they bring them here. Believe me, Jacob, all the children are alive. God willing, they should go on helping us and maybe, Jacob, you too will one day help others."

She took Solly's towel and with the pretense of drying my hair, dabbed at my eyes, pressing my face to her chest. The stolid beating of her heart and the rhythmic rise and fall of her bosom settled me down; she released me and methodically began to dress me. The towel around my waist dropped to the floor, and as if I had been a shop dummy, she slipped the underpants over my nakedness, her hands resting on me for the briefest of moments. "So," she said, "you will do the rest, eh?" Solly was now fully dressed and already swanking around the little room, calling on me to hurry. "Can I have some more soup now?" he asked querulously.

The sound of feet pounding up and down in the corridor outside hastened my need to be fully clothed despite my fear of the clothing's origins. Pants, shirt, and sweater came from three different owners, who, if they weren't dead, as Mrs. Goetz had assured me, I would gladly have done violence to. The shoes were like dead weights on my feet. As Solly and I were shepherded out of the clothes cupboard by Mrs. Goetz, I felt unbearably old, weary, and beaten; I could not span the time from when we were Carmel's "little mannikins" to Mr. Goetz's "younger men."

She marched us briskly down the corridor and into a sunny dining hall where her husband, at the head of a phalanx of children, boys on his right, girls on his left, stood as the titular if not the actual head of the establishment. The tables were covered in pink and blue cloths with a circled monogrammed *A.S.M.H.* in the center. Places were set with a plate, knife, fork, and spoon, and there was a tall jug of milk on each table. Mr. Goetz rang a little handbell, which stilled the buzz of voices.

"*Komm* here to me, Mister Solly and Mister Jacob." He beckoned us to stand in front of him, then, pulling out two chairs, pumped his arms up and down. "Up, up, younger men, zo everybody can see you."

Solly climbed on the chair and beamed around him with obvious enjoyment. It was a long time since he had been the sole center of attention. He straightened his shirt collar, fiddled with his socks, and even put his hands on his hips and smirked. I was disgusted with him and to show it, adopted an ungainly slouch, sinking my hands deep into my trouser pockets. The sun had dropped below the eaves, its rays shone through the big windows, converging on us like a spotlight. I followed them back over the treetops, imagining that I could walk along the rays to freedom.

Mr. Goetz was making a speech. Odd words and many strange names drifted past me. I was almost at the end of the sunbeam, about to descend from the tree to the outside world, when there was a burst of clapping and Mr. Goetz was prodding me to get down from the chair and shake hands with a queue of boys and girls standing gravely surveying me.

Dry hands, small hands, large hands, moist hands, names like Hans, Manfred, Ruti, Erich, Wolfgang, Renate, Anna overwhelmed me. In desperation, I made fists of my hands and thrust them deep in my pockets. The last person to come up to me was a tall redheaded boy with freckles and greenish eyes. He was relaxed and assured.

"Wolfgang," he said softly. "But here it is not a name —I mean in Australia—so I am called Bill. And you, Jacob?"

"Jack," I answered readily. "By jingo, you can call me Jack, eh?"

4

I slept that night between cold sheets drawn so tightly over the mattress that no wrinkle dared to appear. To get into the bed, I had first to exert all my strength to lever the top sheet and blankets out from under the mattress. A monogrammed quilt, heavy as a sandbag, now lay folded precisely in four across my feet. Light floral curtains flapped in a languid breeze; a moonbeam skittering between scudding clouds picked out the humps in the other beds. There were four on each side. In my row, all were occupied. In the other, only one; I knew that beneath that slight hummock, Solly would be lying on his back with one hand stretched out on the pillow. Next to me, Wolfgang/Bill lay at full length, his red hair almost glowing in the half-light. I had taken the last bed in the row. Mr. Goetz had instructed me to occupy it despite my pleading to be next to Solly.

"Ve must fill up der side, young man," he commanded.

"But," I demurred, "but my brother, why can't we . . ."

"It cannot be so."

"Why?"

"Because," and his voice hardened, "ziss is how it must be."

I caught the faintest signal from Bill to desist from further objection, and Solly was propelled at the end of Mr. Goetz's finger to his bed, now the farthest away from mine. And there he slept in pajamas with the trouser legs rolled up and his arm completely enveloped in a striped sleeve. I sensed he really didn't care that much where he slept. Perhaps this was the first of many nights that would follow in which he would slip further and further away from me.

"Bloody German bastard," I swore as Mr. Goetz clomped his way out of the dormitory.

Wolfgang propped himself up on one elbow. "I too am German."

"Go on, you're havin' me on, Bill."

"True, Jack, believe me. From Köln—ach, how do you say it here? Cologne."

"Cologne—like the perfume we nicked from Woolies?"

"Nick—what is nick?"

"Ah, nothing, Bill, forget it." I slid farther down between the stiff white sheets, trying to extract some warmth from their impersonal, harsh weave.

Bill was singing softly to himself: *"Ich hab ein kameraden . . ."* Slowly the sheets accepted my body warmth, and I began to drift off with Mr. Goetz's "Ziss is how it must be" running through my head to the same tune as Bill's song. Then I found I couldn't stop that darn tune. It kept me awake long after Bill's snoring took over. Much later, when I got to know him better and when he had stopped humming the tune (on orders from Mr. Goetz), he told me he had learned it from his uncle, who sang across the trenches to the British in the first world war. Then the Hitler Youth sang it in the streets of Cologne. "They beat us Jew boys up if they caught us," Bill said, and added wistfully, "But gee, it was a beaut song."

I woke next morning to a very strange sight. Bill was standing by his bed. On his forehead was a small black box

44

held in place by leather straps; around his left arm and fingers, leather straps were wound tightly and held in place another black box which fixed to his forearm. A white shawl with striped ends and silken fringes was around his shoulders and on his head a dark velvet skull cap. A prayer book was in his hand, and he swayed in time to a tuneless murmuring. From time to time, he would raise his eyes and look beyond me, through time and space to something I was not privy to. Then it was over. He snapped back to the present, turned to me, and asked: "You didn't lay *tefillin*, Jack?"

I shook my head. He could interpret that how he liked. It could mean that I did not do whatever he said or that I simply didn't know what he was asking me.

As he packed the *tefillin* back in a lovely embroidered velvet bag, he asked me how old I was. Thirteen and a half, I told him. "And you haven't been bar mitzvahed? Well, wait till old Klapper gets hold of you."

"Who's old Klapper?" I was about to ask him, when the thought struck him. "Why were you not bar mitzvahed, Jack?"

What could I tell him? That Father had spoken often about it but feared Carmel's tongue-lashing. "Those old Yid habits," she labeled any feeble effort of Father's to introduce us to his limited knowledge of Judaism. The *mezuzah,* my last link with the Balconies which now nestled safely in my most secret place, had been the cause of terrible rows. Carmel actually feared it, and Father did nothing to assuage that fear—it was perhaps the only hold he ever had over Carmel. As my thirteenth birthday approached, I should have been packed off to the little room behind the Bondi Road synagogue for instruction. There, in company with other boys, some from "good homes," others in sandshoes and thin shorts and sweaters, I would have received lessons in Hebrew, been taught to read a short portion from the Torah scrolls, and ultimately to recite the portion from the pulpit in front of an adoring family. Instead, Solly and I were running messages for the SP bookie and watching the disintegration of our father.

Wolfgang Schlesinger, late of Cologne, Germany, and now the eldest resident of the Abraham Samuelson Memorial Home, took a comb from his locker and ran it through his thick red hair. "I shall help you, Jack," he said. "It is better you should know something—even a little before Klapper starts on you."

All I could think of was the absurd juxtaposition of names that were sent to rule over me. I said out loud, "Out of the Carmel into the Klapper!" I felt a great need then to establish my credentials with Bill. Our ages must have been within months of each other, yet he seemed so much more assured. Even without his clothes, he was much more of a physical presence than I was. I contrasted his stocky, freckled body with my own lightly tanned skinny frame. Yes, I thought, the boys of Cologne were certainly different from the boys of Bondi. As he dressed, I dug deep into the pocket of my pants in my locker. My fingers curled around the tissue paper the *mezuzah* was wrapped in. It was still there, about the thickness of a fountain pen and half as long. My finger found the place where the "eye" was, the place where the Hebrew letter *shin* showed through. This was the full extent of Jewish folklore, ritual, call it what you will, that Father had bequeathed me. I withdrew it slowly from my pocket, let it nestle in the palm of my hand for a moment, then carefully unwrapped it.

"Know what this is, Bill?"

His gray green eyes flickered across my open hand. "Did you nick it, Jack? How else would you have such a thing?"

"It came from our home—first from the real home we had in Bellevue Hill and then . . . then from the dump we lived in before Father . . ." There was going to be plenty of time to explain all that to Bill.

He made no attempt to touch the *mezuzah;* instead he said with cold intensity, "Ours got thrown on the fire—with all my family's books."

"You burnt it?" I asked, aghast.

"Don't you know anything in Australia?" he said, exasperated at my appalling ignorance of life in Cologne in 1939. "The Brownshirts—Nazis—came in broad daylight—"

"Okay, okay," I interrupted him, "so you lost yours, but," I said triumphantly, "Solly and me, we still have ours!" My hand closed around it.

"Look after it" was all Bill said.

The dormitory was now flooded with crisp morning light. Humps became boys who stretched, farted to much laughter, tried to hide erect penises and then turned it into a competition. I looked down the room to Solly's bed. His slight figure made only the barest impression, the tight sheets imprisoning him. I was halfway down the room when the double doors swung open and Mr. Goetz, giving a fair imitation of an army sergeant, called out, "Goot morning, younger men, and how are ve all dis fine day?" There was a great deal of shuffling and a ragged chorus of answers. He turned to me and made a mock bow. "Und how iss our new freund, Jacob? Und where iss his little brother?" He lifted up his hand to shade his eyes as if gazing into a distance. "Ach so-o, der little one is still asleep!"

"I was just going to call him, Mr. Goetz."

But his creaky shoes were already taking strides down the room. I followed close behind, ever ready to protect Solly. German kids I was beginning to understand, but German adults were a different matter. We reached Solly's bedside almost together. Mr. Goetz extended a hairy arm, but I pushed him aside. The last thing Solly needed to wake up to was the moon face and steel-rimmed spectacles of Mr. Goats. I'll say this for old Goats—he stood aside while I ran my fingers through Solly's fine hair and whispered, "Coming for a swim, Solly?" which was the only sure way I knew of getting the little bugger out of bed. At home, he'd spring up, grab his swimsuit and towel, and be halfway down the street before I could catch up with him.

"Too right, Jack," he mumbled now, and his legs were over the bedside in a flash.

"*Wunderbar!*" said Mr. Goetz. "*Sehr gut,* younger man." Whatever it was he said, at least he was smiling.

Solly looked around foolishly, realizing he had been tricked and conscious of his ridiculous appearance in pajamas far too big for him. "We're still in the bad boys' home, aren't we, Jack?"

Mr. Goetz now displayed his authority. "Here we have no bad boys or girls, Solly. Here we only have *kinder*— children —like you to care for. Now, we will all please dress and *komm* to breakfast." He turned to leave, then paused. "But," he waved his finger, "first we shall wash, *nicht wahr?*"

There was a rush for the basins; five boys, three basins, Solly and I hanging back. A boy called Manfred, tubby and already with enough English to make dirty jokes, said: "Ssh, you can hear the girls on the other side pissing." A mad scramble ensued by all except Solly, Bill, and me.

Bill bowed with exaggerated courtesy in imitation of Mr. Goetz and said, "After you, younger men."

Solly headed for the wall but I hauled him back. "The basins, Bill means, you little twerp!"

Bill smiled noncommittally.

The breakfast tables held nothing but the little vases of artificial flowers I had seen the day before. Mrs. Goetz stood sentry by the kitchen door, shepherding boys to one table and girls to another. When we were all seated, she clapped her hands, and one child from each table rose and went to a sideboard to select cutlery and plates.

Manfred nudged me. "Ruti has big tits, eh?" I didn't have to ask which one was Ruti. It was obvious from his crude description that the pleasant, smiling girl who leaned over me and put plate, cutlery, and a glass in front of me could only be Ruti. She wore a school sweater, dark skirt, and knee stockings. As she returned to her place at the table, all I could think of was whether she was wearing a dead girl's clothes. Bill and another girl then rose and went into the kitchen to reappear with trays holding steaming plates of porridge and shiny chrome racks of toast. When all this had been done, Mrs. Goetz sat at the head of the girls' table, and her husband took his place with the boys. Solly ate with noise and enthusiasm; Manfred finished his porridge first and burped. Mr. Goetz waggled a finger at him, yet I thought they shared the same robust sense of humor. If Solly was going to find an ally in this company, I feared, somewhat priggishly, it would be Manfred.

A feeling of loneliness swept over me as I sat at the table. Solly was gorging himself, having, it seemed, found a new star to follow in Manfred. Bill ate each mouthful with careful deliberation while the porridge in my own mouth grew lumpy and distasteful. I had an unreasoning yearning for plain bread with plum jam, for not wearing shoes, and above all to feel the sun on my face. It was out there, the lovely sun, beyond the walls and windows, down the rutted driveway, rising over the Bondi surf. I half rose in my place, my chair scraping noisily on the polished boards.

"You would like something, Jacob?" Mrs. Goetz called out to the kitchen. "Minnie, please to bring some more porridge for der boy."

"Oh shit," I screamed. "I don't want to stay here—with

Germans—with dead boys' clothes—with, with"—I floundered for something else to hate—"with Solly making a pig of himself!"

I tore at my shirt. A button flew off and hit the empty milk jug. The tiny *ping* it made sounded in that deafening silence like a rifle shot. Bill picked it up and with excessive courtesy, placed it on my plate. "It is yours, Jacob, I believe?"

Solly's high-pitched voice, with a deliberately added whine, called out, "He said I was a pig!" Only later did it sink in that Solly had referred to me as *he* and not Jacob, his brother.

Manfred compounded the hurt by allying himself with Solly. "I'm sure he didn't mean it," he said unctuously.

Mr. Goetz, with a wisdom I had not credited him with, leaned forward and said in a conciliatory tone, "Is it all finished now, Jacob?"

I heard footsteps behind me, then felt Mrs. Goetz's large firm hands on my shoulders. She propelled the chair under me and forced me down into it. "Das were goot, younger man. It clears der head and der heart, *nicht wahr?*" She addressed the room: "Now we shall all finish breakfast and get ready for school."

There was a straggly exit from the dining room with Bill assuming the lead as if by right. Ruti led the girls in similar fashion. Since Manfred's gratuitous but nevertheless accurate observation about Ruti, I watched her with a newly awakened interest. As our paths converged and our shoulders nearly touched, she whispered, "I'll sew your button on, Jacob." My heart raced, the back of my neck felt hot; I fingered the front of my shirt where the button was missing. Things were happening in my pants that, right then, I could well have done without.

Solly came up to me. "What's this about school, Jack?"

I said to him roughly, "No buggering about, Solly. We've got to go and that's that. And what's more, I've got to be bar mitzvahed." I caught up with Bill, who already had his satchel slung over his shoulder.

It turned out that Bill and I were going to the nearest technical school, Ruti attended a girls' high school, and, to my dismay, Solly was to go with Manfred and the remaining children to the neighboring state school. We parted at the end of the winding dirt track where it met the asphalt. Bill and Ruti and I waited for a bus; the others walked to the tiny school about a mile from the Abraham Samuelson Memorial Home. I looked out of the bus window; Solly was swaggering along with Manfred, swinging his bag around his head. Any thought I had of calling out to him now seemed quite futile and even unnecessary.

Ruti leaned over the bus seat and remarked on how blond and "un-Jewish" Solly looked. "In Germany, in my home city of Hamburg, he could have walked the streets quite safely—he might even have passed for an Aryan German."

I nodded uncomprehendingly; it had taken me most of my young lifetime to come to grips with the Jew-hating of out-of-work Australian laborers, of a stepmother tied to an unemployable Jew nearly twice her age, of well-meaning policemen who called me Ikey. What in the name of God was an Aryan, I wanted to ask Ruti. Was it a good thing for Solly to be? And what about Bill with his flaming red hair? Could he pass for an Aryan also? Was the color of your hair a passport to freedom from name-calling?

There was such a lot I would have liked to ask Ruti, but not on a school bus and, I suspected, not in front of Bill.

The bus was now laboring up a hill that ran alongside the

51

forbidding wall of the Gladesville Lunatic Asylum. "I've got a barmy aunty in there," I said brightly. Bill and Ruti pointedly avoided looking at the high sandstone wall. "Dad wouldn't take Solly and me to visit her in case they kept us there." I waited for the laugh that should have followed. The pair of them were sitting with arms folded and eyes straight ahead.

Ruti turned her head slightly and said, "I do not think you will ever see your aunt again, Jacob." The bus slid into the stop to let Ruti off. As she gathered up her bag to alight, she leaned over to me, her hair brushing my face. "My uncle was taken in the middle of the night to such a place by the SS; we never saw him again, either."

I watched her mingle with the other girls on the street; she was different, already with the deportment of an older person, not graceful, not gauche—just older than her fifteen years. There were tangents in my life that seemed to touch hers. I took a school atlas from my bag; just looking at the map of Germany seemed to bring us closer together. I nudged Bill to show me where Hamburg was. "Later," he said. "We're nearly at the Tech, Jack. You'll be in first year, and I'm in second year. Give them the letter from Mr. Goetz and don't worry. I'll meet you in the shelter shed at lunchtime."

My first few months in the Home were a mixture of pain and pleasure, of resentment and acquiescence, of loneliness and jealousy, of acceptance and rejection. The routine of the place had removed from my shoulders the responsibility for day-to-day survival and, with it, the care of Solly. He became Mrs. Goetz's "little mannikin," a term that filled me with loathing. I had visions of Solly forever being someone's little mannikin, a fox-terrier puppy that could tear the clothes from the line and receive nothing more than a playful slap.

He put on weight, he got first pick at the secondhand-clothes cupboard so that he always looked so much more at home in the castoffs than the rest of us. He was given the easier tasks on the job roster and even then managed to get Manfred to do the ones he liked least. Those two were inseparable, Solly having persuaded Mr. Goetz to change Manfred's bed so the two of them were now side by side. He taught Manfred the vernacular of the Bondi streets, which Manfred, a year older than he, coupled with the ribald humor of his former Vienna suburb.

Bill still rose every weekday morning and put on his *tefillin* and said his prayers. On Saturday, or the Sabbath, as he patiently explained to me, one doesn't put on the *tefillin,* as it could be interpreted as doing a form of work. Saturday, one went to the synagogue, heard the reading of the Law, and, if one had been bar mitzvahed, actually participated by being invited to read from the scrolls—the first five books of the Bible set out in Hebrew and handwritten on parchment. I watched him one Sabbath as he mounted the steps of the reading desk, his prayer shawl around his shoulders, an embroidered skullcap on his red hair. In a clear voice, he read from the scrolls, then with a dramatic gesture lifted them up by their handles high above his head and turned them around for all the congregation to see. The old men at the desk then took the scrolls from him and warmly shook his hand. Bill returned to his seat beside me. "You see, Jack, this is an honor. You are reckoned to be a man when you are called up to the Torah like that."

Mr. Klapper, my Hebrew teacher, charged with preparing me for my bar mitzvah, sat next to me. He patted me on the knee. "*Nu,* my boy, it won't be long before your turn will come."

He came to the Home twice a week to instruct me, took a glass of schnapps "to clear der troat," then rehearsed me in the musical notes of the portion I would have to recite before the congregation. He used a beautifully fashioned silver pointer shaped like a forefinger, no bigger than a pennib, to point out the place to me. "In Poland," he said, "I was a *Chazan*—ach, how do you say it here? A reader in the synagogue. It is a profession." He shook his head. "Ah well, in Australia, I am just a teacher of boys—also an honorable profession," he added hastily. He was a decent man who smelt of musty books and pungent alcohol subjugated by peppermints. Once, he cut our lesson short. "I have a *mitzvah* to perform, Jacob," he confided. "Do you know what is a *mitzvah?*" I shook my head. "A *mitzvah* is a good deed. This afternoon I am going to perform a *brith*—circumcision." He reached into his long coat and withdrew a silver case. Inside, on the velvet lining lay small surgical instruments. "As Abraham circumcised Isaac, I shall bring a newborn baby boy into the covenant of Abraham." Poor, unsuspecting Mr. Klapper! He left me with a nightmare that went on for months.

A Saturday in August, three months or so from now, had been fixed as the date for my bar mitzvah. Mrs. Pearlman arrived one afternoon and commanded me to appear before her. She pinched and prodded me and declared that I had grown up since she had brought us here. "Almost a man, eh, Jacob? And that's what I want to talk to you about. Who would you like to ask to your bar mitzvah—from your family, I mean?"

Who indeed! When father had married Carmel, his family had thenceforth ignored him. Our mother's family, storekeepers in a western New South Wales town, had not forgiven Carmel for marrying their former son-in-law and thereafter maintained only the most tenuous of contacts. That left Uncle Siddy. Mrs. Pearlman was droning on about having all the children in the home present and, of course, Mr. and

54

Mrs. Goetz. She herself would also be there. She might even be able to persuade some of the Committee to come, she said —although, you know, Jacob, they are such busy people.

"I want our Uncle Siddy to come, more than anyone else."

Mrs. Pearlman was prepared for this. She put a hand over mine. "I suppose, Jacob, you've been wondering why Mr. Kaiser hasn't been to visit you?"

"Not really. I know he's in the country buying scrap gold like he used to do with Father."

"He hasn't written to you, has he?"

"Too busy, I suppose," I said defensively. I withdrew my hand from hers.

"I'm sorry to tell you that your Uncle Siddy is in jail." She stood up and smoothed her dress. "It would be better if you did not see him again."

"But that's not forever, is it, Mrs. Pearlman? I mean, people do get out of jail. There's ages to go before I'm bar mitzvahed. Maybe Uncle Siddy will get out by then." Belatedly I thought to ask, "What has he done?"

"Well I suppose you might as well have the truth, Jacob. Mr. Kaiser found the man who was your stepmother's ah, friend—the time-payment man—and er, he, well, he assaulted him so badly he put him in the hospital."

Good on Uncle Siddy! Bloody wonderful! At last there was some justice in the world. I could just picture that sleek mongrel in a hospital bed swathed in bandages and plaster.

"Mmm, that's not good, is it, Mrs. Pearlman?" Let her figure out which I meant—the assault or that Uncle Siddy was in jail. Out of the window, I could see Solly hanging upside down from a parallel bar. He and Manfred were egging a girl on to do the same. While it was all right for me to feel proud about Uncle Siddy beating up that swine and even being in jail for it, it was quite a different matter to tell Solly, who would trumpet it far and wide. I would pitch him a yarn that Uncle Siddy was way up north on business.

Mrs. Pearlman was rabbiting on about getting me a new suit for the bar mitzvah. "Well, maybe not quite new, Jacob. I happen to know that Eric, our treasurer's son, has outgrown his bar mitzvah suit, and he's just about your size."

I gritted through clenched teeth, "Don't forget to ask if he's finished with his shoes too, Mrs. Pearlman." As a final thrust at her, I called her to the window. The girl was now hanging upside down from the bars, her skirt over her head. Solly and Manfred were doubled up with laughter. Mrs. Pearlman glanced briefly at them and to my surprise made no comment. She linked her arm in mine and asked me to escort her to her car. As she settled behind the wheel and pulled on her gloves, she said, "Being bar mitzvahed gives you responsibilities of manhood, and that includes seeing your young brother stays out of trouble. Do you understand me, Jacob?" She let the clutch out savagely, and the car shot off, shaving the trees overhanging the drive.

Bill was aimlessly dribbling a soccer ball over the rough ground. After the dust of Mrs. Pearlman's departure had settled, he maneuvered the ball to my feet to stop dead in front of me and stood with one foot on it as though it was a trophy he had won. "I played center forward for our team at the Gymnasium," he said. I looked blankly at him. He explained that, in Germany, a Gymnasium was the high school. He nodded his head down the driveway. "What did she want, Jack?" He rolled the ball onto the toe of his shoe and kicked it into his arms.

I said, "Has anyone in your family ever been in jail, Bill?"

"Why do you ask?"

"Have they?"

"Well, sort of."

56

"What does that mean?"

"He didn't do anything wrong, like stealing or things like that."

"Who?"

Bill dropped the ball and sat on it. With his finger he drew in the dust a square with bars. "My uncle—my mother's brother. They said he was a communist."

"Is that bad—like beating somebody up?" I asked hopefully.

Bill shrugged. "I don't really know. Uncle Joachim used to go around sticking up posters. My father warned him about that, and once he gave me a hiding for helping him." He kicked the ball high in the air and headed it. "Come on, Jack, you can be goalie, and I've got to get it past you."

I positioned myself between two struggling saplings while Bill dribbled the ball to within a few yards of me, then shot with great accuracy. Mr. Goetz came out and joined us. Bill passed the ball to him, he shot it back, and before I knew it they were shouting "goal!" Solly and Manfred, attracted by the shouting, joined in. Solly picked up the ball and ran with it. There were cries of "foul!" from Bill and Mr. Goetz.

"Tackle him!" I yelled. Manfred lumbered after Solly but had no hope of catching him.

Solly, in true Rugby style, veered round behind the goalposts and triumphantly deposited the ball on the ground. "How's that for a try!" he told the dumbfounded Goetz and Bill.

Manfred rolled on the ground in near hysterics. "Oh, will we ever teach these two how to play soccer," he gasped.

The game broke up as the stooped, black-coated figure of Mr. Klapper limped up the driveway. I was about to have my last bar mitzvah lesson before the great day.

5

Haazinu is the Hebrew word opening Chapter 32 of Deuteronomy: "Give ear, ye heavens, and I will speak."

The portion of the Torah that I had learned was designated by this opening word. At nearly fourteen years of age, nine months later than was usual, I would have the effrontery to stand before a congregation and recite the final admonitory words of Moses as he castigated his errant people. Mr. Klapper had constant recourse to his bottle of schnapps as he tutored me in harmonics and reading. The thick and thin Hebrew lettering blurred before my eyes, my voice refused to emulate his reedy example. Some of his teaching I retained. I loved the dietary laws, with their references to aromatic spices and ingredients like something out of the Arabian Nights. I could now recite the morning prayer as perfectly as Bill, and I loved the all-enveloping safety of the prayer shawl. Never mind that it was not new, that it was redolent of mothballs, that the gold embroidery now hung in ragged slivers.

Wonder of wonders! The suit obtained by Mrs. Pearlman fit me well. On the breast pocket I could still see the stitch marks where a school badge had been removed. It reeked of dry-cleaning fluid, and as I was about to put the *mezuzah* in the pants pocket, I discovered a fair-sized hole.

Mrs. Goetz, who rarely entered the boys' dormitory, came to inspect me. "Ve are zo proud of you, younger man, are ve not, Bertold?" She reached into her overall pocket and produced a white handkerchief still in a cellophane wrap. It was the only new thing that I had on me for this great day.

It was the last Saturday in August. All the children of the Abraham Samuelson Memorial Home were decked out in their (or somebody's) best clothes. The girls, like spring flowers, appeared in pretty floral print dresses with precautionary cardigans thrown insouciantly over their shoulders. The Goetzes wore the last of their former Berlin finery, heavy dark woven suits. Mrs. Goetz's was so severe in style that it could easily have been interchangeable with the one her husband wore. Solly had caught a cold during the week. Ruti had been delegated to look after him, a task she performed with just enough affection to make me quite jealous. Mr. Goetz consulted his pocket watch, gave a signal to his wife who set her pistonlike legs in motion, and the entire ménage fell in behind her, maintaining this formation on and off bus and tram until it reached the entrance to the Great Synagogue of Sydney.

Mrs. Goetz shepherded the girls upstairs to the ladies' gallery. Downstairs, in the main hall of the synagogue, three seats in the front pew had been left especially for Mr. Goetz, Solly, and me. It was a beautiful building with a high vaulted ceiling painted sky blue, with thousands of stars. Directly in front of me was the massive, elevated reading desk and behind that, in a proscenium arch like a theater and covered with embroidered plum-red curtains, stood the Holy Ark. Later in the Sabbath morning service, the curtains would part to reveal a number of Torah scrolls clothed in embroidered mantles and bearing silver breastplates. Hanging from the handles of the scrolls were the same delicate silver pointers that Mr. Klapper used.

The office holders of the synagogue sat in splendid isolation in boxes on either side of the reading desk. They wore top hats and morning suits and, over them, their prayer shawls. From the viewpoint of a thirteen-and-a-half-year-old, they looked like severe bloodless men without pity. Yet I recognized one of them as a benefactor of the Abraham Samuelson Memorial Home, a jovial enough man who came once a month in a big car, accompanied by his son, and toured the Home distributing candies, much to the annoyance of Mrs. Goetz. He nodded his shiny topper ever so slightly in acknowledgment of my presence. A long way off, in a side pew, I saw Bill, and despite a warning elbow from Mr. Goetz, I turned around and caught sight of Ruti, up there among the stars.

Suddenly Mr. Goetz was hoisting me to my feet. "You are next, Jacob," he hissed. The beadle was at the end of the pew beckoning me to follow him.

Solly whispered, "Good on yer, Jack!" I squeezed passed the knees, came to the end of the pew, and found myself in the aisle, facing the flight of steps that led to the reading desk. The flowing black gown of the beadle preceded me until, suddenly, there I was, in front of the great desk, the scrolls before me. I was flanked by two rabbis. One bent down and produced a footstool for me to stand on. Just as well; without it, my chin rested on the desk! One rabbi passed the other a note. He read it, tucked it up the sleeve of his black gown, then with a sonorous voice, called out my Hebrew name—Yakov ben Pinchas Ha-Levi.

For one glorious moment in my life, I was not merely Jack Kaiser, son of Felix Kaiser. No! I was a descendant, through a history I barely understood, of the tribe of the Levites, and I was the son of Pinchas who was the son of Gideon who was the son of . . . I was truly somebody with a past, even with a prospect of a future. But now the scrolls were unrolled in front of me, and the silver pointer was poised for me to commence my portion.

"*Zocher,*" I began, and from there on, the melody flowed out of me for what seemed like eternity but was in fact only a few minutes. Six verses, and my moment of glory had passed. The scrolls were rolled up, I read one further blessing, and it was all over. There were polite murmurs of approval, and I was shepherded down the other side of the reading desk and back to my seat in the pew.

The service continued, but from there on I took no part in it. I sat between Solly and Mr. Goetz in a miasma of contentment. I forgave the rabbi who sermonized about the unbounded charity of the benefactors of the Abraham Samuelson Memorial Home who had "rescued so many of our brethren from the death camps of Europe." Perhaps he was not familiar with the sons of fathers who had been pushed off the cliffs of Bondi.

Solly was sniffling with his cold. The last hymn of the service had been sung, men were removing their prayer shawls, shaking hands with acquaintances, and wishing everyone in sight a good Sabbath. Mr. Goetz stood up and signaled to his wife in the gallery. Once more, we were an orderly assembled group on the pavement outside the synagogue, isolated from outsiders and insulated from contact by the shepherding skills of the Goetzes.

I found myself alongside Ruti. In the brilliant spring sunshine, she looked lovelier than anything I could imagine. "Such a fine name you have, Jack," she said. "Yakov ben Pinchas—and of the tribe of Levi." She took my face in her hands and kissed me on the lips.

In that instant I felt dizzy, shaken, cold, hot, embarrassed, and proud. Manfred's sniggering went unnoticed. The people surrounding us seemed to melt away, and Ruti and I were alone in the middle of that jostling throng. I felt for her hand, and it closed gently around mine. Solly was tugging at her sleeve, his nose streaming. I pulled out the new handkerchief that Mrs. Goetz had given me. The *mezuzah* came out with it and made a tinny ringing sound as it hit the pavement. As I picked it up, Ruti said, "What a strange thing to be carrying around with you, Jack."

I pressed it into her hand. "Would you like it?"

Solly snatched it away from her. "You can't have it because it belongs to Jack and me!"

Ruti was unperturbed by this. She laughed and said, "Well, perhaps someday, Jack, we'll all share it." The moment was over; she busied herself organizing our departure for the Home. Watching her, I thought, bar mitzvah, manhood, call it what you like, I would never be as grown-up as Ruti.

On the 3rd of September, 1939, a week or so after my bar mitzvah, Australia joined England in declaring war on Germany. A few days after that, two Australian military policeman arrived at the Home and took Mr. Goetz away. It was a time of bewildering excitement and constant change. Poor, benign Bertold Goetz, displaced defender of German culture, former Berlin accountant, and for a brief time in charge of a Jewish children's home, was now an enemy alien. He languished for a while in a detention camp in the wheatbelt of New South Wales only to reappear as a sergeant in an Australian army unit loading military supplies for Darwin.

A tramp steamer left Trieste in early 1940 and after a ten-week voyage that took it to Sydney via the Panama Canal, arrived at Circular Quay with four hundred Jewish refugees on board. They had found their way here from the falling cities of Europe from that last free port of embarkation.

Many of them had not seen their children for over a year. An international child-welfare agency had garnered the children, like a failing but valuable crop, and dispersed them to Canada, England, and Australia.

Among the Trieste steamer's passengers were the parents of Wolfgang, Ruti, and Manfred. Their common plight had united them on the voyage in the face of the crew's disinterest in their well-being as effectively as the Nazis who had confiscated their property. The women stood at the head of the gangplank, drawing their tatty fur coats about them despite the warmth of the morning. The husbands, looking incongruous in velour hats and long dark coats, daringly loosened their ties only to be chided by their wives for failing to observe the correct standards of dress, as befitted European sophisticates arriving in such a gauche country as Australia.

Down below, the wharf laborers in blue undershirts and battered felt hats pushed well back on their heads, mistook them for Italians and called out to the women, "Dona squeeza da tomato!"

A sling went over the ship's side. The refugees watched apprehensively as their last remaining possessions hit the wharf with a thud. Self-important Jewish officials went on board, voices were raised, hands flew in the air, and finally the tall, red-haired figure of Mr. Willi Schlesinger led the bewildered group ashore. For reasons which I could not then fathom, I had shut out any interest in the parents of Bill, Ruti, and Manfred. Childish jealousy it may have been, but I could not bear their repetitive stories of parental indulgence, their isolation from what I considered the real world. There were even moments when I found myself pleased when, through Nazi actions, their pleasures were restricted. I found myself taking a perverse pleasure in telling exaggerated tales of our life in Bondi, of the Carmel era. Solly backed me up to the hilt, strutting around boasting about his familiarity with police cars and how we robbed the milko of his milk. We built Uncle Siddy up into a figure of Robin Hood status. We did not have any photographs to show of our father and mother, unlike the others who all had little wallets of pictures that opened out concertina-fashion to show entire families, including grandparents.

And now they were about to be reunited, if not with entire families, at least with their parents. A letter on official Abraham Samuelson Memorial Home letterhead, signed by Mrs. Pearlman, was posted on the notice board.

The Committee is pleased to announce the safe arrival in Sydney of the parents of the following children who are resident in the Home:

Willi and Clara Schlesinger, parents of Wolfgang.
Henry and Irma Kahn, parents of Ruti.
Mitzi Strauss, mother of Manfred.

They will be permitted to visit the children in the Home this Sunday afternoon at 2 P.M.
By order of the Board, Mrs. R. Pearlman, Secretary.

Bill read it with his usual measured calm. He announced, "My father will arrive precisely on time. He will be wearing his homburg hat, and he will carry his briefcase. He will shake my hand and say, 'How goes it, Wolfgang? Is all in order with you?' My mother will kiss me on the cheek and probably tell me that I have grown."

I had no reason to disbelieve him. Bill being Bill—or momentarily reverting to his alter ego, Wolfgang—was right on most matters.

Ruti's eyes were swimming in tears. She read the notice

over and over, pulling up her socks, pulling down her jumper, combing her hair with her fingers. Nicest of all, she took my arm and squeezed my hand. "Is it not wonderful, Jack?" I felt myself getting warm all over. It certainly was wonderful to have her hand locked in mine, to feel her breast against my arm. "Tomorrow they come. We will be together again and . . ."

". . . and you'll leave here, and I'll never see you again, Ruti."

Bill edged us aside and pointed to the notice. He ran his finger down it and stopped at the name of Mitzi Strauss. "I do not see here the name of Manfred's father."

A chill came over our little group. We recalled the photographs of Mr. Strauss, a sturdy man pictured against a snow-capped mountain. He was wearing shorts and heavy walking shoes and carried a stick. Manfred had boasted how his father had climbed the Matterhorn. Nobody believed him then. Now I felt a twinge of conscience—maybe he had.

To break the tension, I said, "I reckon the bugger's stuck on that bloody mountain, and he'll come on later."

Bill and Ruti, from some inner knowledge I was not privy to, shook their heads in disbelief. "They've got him, Jack," Bill said gravely. He turned to Ruti. "Shall you tell Manfred or shall I?"

I walked away and stood on the verandah. In the distance, I could see Solly still trying to force a goal past Manfred. They fought over the ball and rolled on the ground like pups squabbling. Without the ordered discipline of Mr. Goetz, those two were continually in trouble. Manfred had an insatiable appetite for food and stole from the pantry while Solly kept watch for him. And now Bill strode across the grass, forced the two boys apart, and was speaking to Manfred. I could hear Manfred shouting "bloody liar," but underlying it there was already a discernible note of acceptance.

Solly kicked the ball disconsolately, then came over to me. "What d'yer reckon, Jack?" he said in a puzzled voice. "Is it worse than being pushed off a cliff?"

These days, Mrs. Goetz's moods varied with the letters she received from her husband. They came in brown army envelopes with sticky tape along one edge where they had been opened, read by a censor, and resealed. She was also embarrassed at having to ask me to read them for her. Mr. Goetz had been forced to write them in English so that the army censor could read them. This fact, together with the censor's obliterations of Mr. Goetz's attempts to describe his life as a uniformed laborer in the Australian army, made them almost unintelligible. As the months wore on, his written English improved to the point where he used a swearword Mrs. Goetz was quite unfamiliar with. She folded the letter so that only a few words including the swearword showed. "What is this 'flaming' sergeant, Jacob?" She saw me squirming. "Aha, younger man, I can tell it is something not nice, *nicht wahr?*"

For the two days before the Sunday referred to in Mrs. Pearlman's letter, she was in a storm. Something from her husband's new military career had rubbed off on her, and she stamped about the Home issuing orders, clothing, and demands for our cleanliness that far exceeded her usual Germanic requirements. By noon on Sunday, everyone was in a highly nervous state, not least because of the dose of senna pods administered the night before so that we would have inner cleanliness as well. I had pleaded that as Solly and I were not expecting parental visits, it was not fair that we too should be dosed.

Bill was right. A minute or so before two o'clock that fine spring April Sunday, we heard the familiar groaning of Mrs. Pearlman's car. Like an uneven picket fence, we were lined up on the verandah, clad in the very best the secondhand-clothes cupboard could supply for this important reunion. Solly and Manfred stood together, as different as chalk and cheese but now closely united by their newfound common bond. Perhaps Manfred had suggested to him that they could share Mitzi Strauss between them. Mrs. Goetz positively creaked in her starched uniform; she actually stood to attention as the car swept around the last bend in the track.

There was a moment of comedy as the car halted at the top of the driveway. Mrs. Pearlman's gloved hand was out of the window, trying to wrench the door open. It would not budge. "Damn thing's broken," she shouted through the window. The rear door opened. The tall, unmistakable figure of Mr. Willi Schlesinger unwound itself. He took one step to the recalcitrant door, turned the handle, opened the door, and bowed to the exasperated Mrs. Pearlman.

"Gnadige Frau," he murmured courteously, "please to get out now."

Mrs. Goetz advanced to meet her. But Mrs. Pearlman almost landed at her feet. Right behind her was the roly-poly, volatile, bouncy, bubbling Mitzi Strauss, pushing wispy Mrs. Pearlman aside in her rush to reach her Manfred. She swept him up, smothered him in lipstick, hugged him to her, and filled the air with the most infectious laughter ever heard in the Abraham Samuelson Memorial Home.

The formality that Mrs. Goetz had wished for the afternoon (no doubt in deference to her absent Bertold) was shattered. Mr. Schlesinger looked at his watch, then shook hands with his son, passed him over to his mother, who for a moment appeared as though she might embrace him, thought better of it, and kissed him on the cheek. They both possessed the stature of the Cologne cathedral, a building they had always admired but never entered.

Mr. Schlesinger went up to Ruti. "You are Ruth Kahn, I think? Come with me to the car. Your father needs a little help." They returned together to the car. He reached in, then backed out, almost carrying Henry Kahn, a pale, white-haired man whose suit hung slackly over his meager frame. He set him on his feet in front of Ruti, then Irma Kahn emerged from the car and put a walking stick in her husband's hand. The three of them stood beside the car like a self-supporting triangle held together by love. It was impossible to hear what they said. They made no attempt to join the others on the verandah; Henry, Irma, and Ruti Kahn were in a private world of their own.

Watching them, I felt an unreasoning resentment at not being a part of that family; I would even have accepted the weakly Henry Kahn as a substitute father—anything to be constantly in the company of Ruti, who, as I observed her with longing, was obviously the strongest one in that little group. It was her arms that enveloped the other two, comforting and reassuring them. I turned to look at Bill. He was a mirror image of his father. His mother stood by his side and seemed to be awaiting orders from his father. I wanted to tell Solly my thoughts; I needed him, as family, to confide in. From the dining room, his giggling, punctuated by Mitzi's arch admonitions to him to behave, fell on my ears like intrusive, unwanted music.

This emotion-charged scene of families being reunited, together with the senna-pod dosing, had put a dreadful strain on my bowels. I also felt a driving desire to do something utterly unacceptable, to destroy the momentary happiness that surrounded but excluded me. I left the verandah and ran over to where Mrs. Pearlman had parked the car. At the top of my voice, I yelled out: "That bloody senna tea is giving me the runs, Mrs. Goetz."

From somewhere behind me, a voice answered, "Stick a cork up your arse, Jacob!"

A man emerged from behind the car, lifted me high in the air, and sat me down hard on the car hood.

"Uncle Siddy, you beauty," I yelled exultantly. "Where the hell did you spring from—how did you find us—what are you doing here—why aren't you in . . ."

He flipped his hat to the back of his head. "Steady on, hold hard there, Jake, first things first. I thought you were bustin' to go to the dunny?" With one hand on my shoulder, he sauntered nonchalantly to the verandah steps. "Now, Jake, you go about your business, and I'll find out who's the head sherang around here."

The shock of seeing Uncle Siddy appear out of the blue was almost more than the strain on my bowels could stand. I tore away from him, past the little clumps of Schlesingers and Kahns, dodged Mrs. Goetz's outstretched hand, and shouted to Solly as I flew down the corridor to the toilets, "Uncle Siddy's come, Solly—dinkum, he's here!"

I caught a glimpse of Solly's chocolate-covered face as I flashed past. The little bugger was sitting on Mitzi Strauss's knee like a big booby, letting her stuff him and Manfred with the contents of her bulging handbag.

When I finally reappeared, feeling shaky but decidedly more at ease, I had merely to follow the voices to locate Uncle Siddy. His broad Australian accent cut through the continental voices like a band saw let loose in an orchestra. Mrs. Goetz's arms flew in all directions as she tried to conduct a conversation with the rapid-fire torrent that was Uncle Siddy trying to tell her that "the two dinky-di little nippers you've got here are me nephews, the sons of me late brother Felix—may he rest in peace!"

Mrs. Goetz had given up and flopped in a chair. "Ach,"

she moaned, "I wish my Bertold was here now—he speaks Australian, from der army he has learned it—such words!"

She was saved from further frustration by Mrs. Pearlman, who confronted Uncle Siddy as calmly as though she had seen him only yesterday. "I do not think it very wise of you to come here, Mr. Kaiser."

"What? Not visit me own flesh an' blood? Come on, Rosie Pearlman, you ought ter know me better than that."

Mrs. Pearlman motioned to me to leave them. Uncle Siddy canceled her instruction by gripping a handful of the back of my coat. He treated Mrs. Pearlman to his most benign smile and said, "You're poor Normie Pearlman's widow, aren't you?"

Rosie Pearlman actually simpered; she drew a hankie from her sleeve and nodded. Siddy pulled himself erect in imitation of a military bearing. "Gave his life for his country, Jake, that's what poor old Normie did—in France, wasn't it, Rosie?"

Uncle Siddy was scoring points, he was on a winning streak and wasn't about to let up. "Now hop it, Jake, and fetch young Solly."

There was no need. Mitzi Strauss was floating toward us like a slice of rich Vienna cream-cake. On either hand, like the top and bottom layers, were Solly and Manfred. Her perfume preceded her, as cloying as a night in a botanical hothouse. It completely swamped the delicate cologne on Rosie Pearlman's hankie.

And it had a most extraordinary effect on Uncle Siddy. Like the mustard gas which had laid poor Normie low, the perfume that Mitzi Strauss exuded nearly floored Sidney Kaiser—my uncle, who could beat up a slick-haired door-to-door salesman, who had done a stretch at The Bay, who had defied and beguiled the fibrous Mrs. Pearlman. His hat came off with a sweep, he buttoned up his coat, pulled his gut in, stuck out his hand, and said hoarsely, "G'day!"

Solly ruined it. He grabbed Uncle Siddy's outstretched hand and yelled, "Did you bring us any busted watches to play with, Uncle Siddy?"

"Ah, so you remember, do you, you little tiger." He squeezed Solly's hand and when he released it, a shilling lay in his palm. "There's a deener for you, Solly, me boy, and here's another for your little cobber."

Mrs. Pearlman, disgusted at such generosity to small boys, flounced off to inform Mrs. Goetz. I too could have done with a share of Uncle Siddy's openhandedness; instead, in my best grown-up "now I am bar mitzvahed and come-of-age" manner, I formally introduced Mrs. Mitzi Strauss of Vienna, Austria, to Mr. Sidney Kaiser, uncle of Jacob and Solly Kaiser, once of Bellevue Hill, later of Bondi, and now residents of the Abraham Samuelson Memorial Home.

Mitzi Strauss nervously extended her hand. Perhaps she half expected to find a coin in it. "I am Frau Strauss," she started to say, then with a little shrug she beamed at Siddy. "Ach, what does it matter, here in Australia? I am Mitzi—please to call me Mitzi."

The sun came out from behind the treetops. Even the magpies' harsh call seemed softened at that moment. Solly and Manfred watched the two adults closely. Sensing there would be no clash, they ran off, richer by a shilling each and whatever else might flow from the meeting.

Siddy said, "Pleased to meetcha, Mitzi. That nipper of yours, whatsisname, Manfred, is it? He's good mates with Solly, isn't he?" He turned to me, nudging me with his elbow. "And what about you, Jake? A grownup fella like you must be lookin' for girls now, eh?"

I felt a shiver of dislike for Uncle Siddy. In the distance I could see Ruti still closeted with her parents. With all the judgmental brutality of my age, I compared their self-sustaining gentle warmth with the extroverted, will-to-survive, rough-and-tumble attitude to life of Mitzi Strauss and Sidney Kaiser. I longed to be the man in Ruti's family, to take the place of her sickly father and thereby achieve a status that I could never have if I lived in the shadow of Uncle Siddy and, who knows, the effervescent Mitzi Strauss.

The two of them were getting on like a house on fire. Questions flew back and forth interspersed with gales of laughter. It was obvious that Mitzi Strauss had quickly informed Siddy that there was no chance of Mr. Strauss ever coming to Australia. From that disclosure onward, they strolled around the grounds, arms linked, occasionally looking back when Uncle Siddy would call out to me to verify a point in whatever tale he was pitching Mitzi Strauss.

As we neared the verandah, I detached myself from them and leaned disconsolately against the wall a few feet away from the Kahns. There was no laughter from them, no outward sign of joyful reunion, and yet something reached out to me (or was it something in me reaching out to them?) that drew me into their group while I yet remained apart. Mrs. Kahn, gray from her tightly drawn-back hair to her dusty flat-heeled shoes, reminded me of one of the convent order of the Gray Sisters whom I had often seen picking up the winos as they lay in the sand at dusk on Bondi Beach. Her shoulders seemed perpetually bent, ever ready to minister to the needy. As she stooped over her husband, I wondered if she also had the same courage as those nuns.

Suddenly she straightened up and said something sharply to Ruti. They were helping Henry Kahn to his feet. Ruti beckoned me to join them. Without bothering to introduce me to her parents, she said in an urgent, commanding voice, "Jacob, my father is not well. He needs to go to the toilet. Will you please accompany him." And as an afterthought, "He speaks quite good English, you know."

Henry Kahn, a dried twig of a man, laid a feathery arm on mine. I steered him down the corridor in silence, popped him into a cubicle, and turned a tap on over the basin full-force to disguise the sick man's retching. I did not inquire how he was. I splashed water over my face, turned the tap off, and took a leak. There was now silence from Mr. Kahn's cubicle. I dried my hands on the roller towel, taking far longer than needed. Still they felt clammy, and my heart seemed as though it was being squeezed into a small corner of my chest. Breathing deeply, I called out in a voice not wanting to be heard or indeed answered, "You okay in there, Mr. Kahn?"

There was a faint trickling sound from the cistern—and that was all.

I had to look. After all, Ruti had given her father into my care. I had no wish to see Mr. Kahn dead on a dunny seat in the Abraham Samuelson Memorial Home. But if he was sick enough to merely remove him from the pivotal position in their family, I would be happy. I was honest enough to be appalled but not deterred by the coldness of my reasoning and how the thought gave rise, even at this moment, to planning our future life together, Ruti's and mine, without Mr. Kahn.

I walked toward the swinging double doors of the bathroom. I could hear whistling coming from the other side. I stopped. Nobody in the Abraham Samuelson Memorial Home whistled "Lily of Laguna." Uncle Siddy, hands in pockets, pushed the door open with his boot.

"Ah, there, Jake, just waterin' the horse, was ya?"

I grabbed him by the arm. "See that dunny there, Uncle Siddy? There's a bloke in there, and he's real sick or maybe even dead or something."

"Go on, you don't say?"

"Dinkum, Uncle Siddy. Have a look for yourself if you don't believe me."

I pushed open the cubicle door. It caught on Henry

74

Kahn's leg and stuck fast. I freed his leg, and his sticklike body fell off the seat and lay in a crumpled heap on the tiles. There were vomit and blood down the front of his suit.

Siddy looked quizzically at poor Mr. Kahn. "Well, that's one for the books, I must say, young Jake. It don't say much for the food around here, does it?" He looked at me long and hard, then bent down and took Mr. Kahn's thin wrist in his hairy hand. "Well, he's still hangin' on, Jake, but only just this side of handin' in his chips, I'd say. Y' didn't try an' do 'im in, didja?"

I watched him slide the limp figure out of the cubicle; I was frozen with fright at the implication of his jokey remark.

Siddy laid Mr. Kahn on the tiles. "Know who he is, Jake?"

"It's Ruti's—it's Mrs. Kahn's husband. One of the reffo parents that came here to visit today. They came in Mrs. Pearlman's car."

Siddy put his arm around my shoulders and led me out of the bathroom. I was surprised to see that it was still daylight, that all the normal sounds of people and children still went on. Mrs. Goetz was obviously impatient at the day's interruption to her routine. She was rounding up the parents like a sheepdog, edging them toward Mrs. Pearlman's car. Willi and Clara Schlesinger had clearly said all they had to say necessary to Bill and stood waiting impassively for the moment of departure. Mitzi Strauss, looking a trifle disheveled, wagged her finger at the approach of Uncle Siddy who, ignoring her, strode straight past to where Ruti and her mother sat together like two travelers waiting for the last train to God knows where.

They stood up and eyed Siddy suspiciously. He scratched his head, stuck one foot up on the bench, and said, "Now, ladies, which of youse speaks English?"

Ruti ignored him. She grabbed my arm. "Jacob, please,

where is my father? You have been gone such a long time. I would have looked for you, but that silly Mrs. Strauss—"

"Steady on there, miss," Siddy interrupted.

Mrs. Kahn eyed him nervously. "Whom is this man?" she asked.

With little pride now, I replied miserably that he was my uncle.

Siddy, suddenly aware that he had lost an ally and smarting at Ruti's reference to Mitzi Strauss, said in a matter-of-fact tone, "I think the old bloke near cashed in his chips in there, missus."

The two of them looked blankly to me for an explanation. Ruti let go of my arm, picked up her father's walking stick, and gripped it until her knuckles were white.

"I know what he means, *Mutti*," she said softly. "He is telling us that Papa is near death." She repeated the word for *dead* in German, three or four times. They sat down and Ruti waved Siddy away and at the same time pulled me down beside her. The sorrow that flowed through Ruti and her mother reached me like a tide that washed around and over the three of us. If ever I was going to be a member of that family, this would be the moment. Ruti and her mother were grieving, but I felt reborn.

Toward the end of 1940, the Abraham Samuelson Memorial Home for Jewish Children was requisitioned by the government for use as a training center for army nurses. The committee of the Home, led by the resourceful and indefatigable Rosie Pearlman, persuaded one of the Jewish community's leading citizens to vacate his North Shore mansion to provide alternative accommodation for the growing number of children who arrived at Circular Quay. Some came with parents, some forlornly hoping that the remnants of their scattered families would eventually follow them to Australia, a country they could not have pointed to on a map some months earlier.

The enormous Spanish-mission-style house, set in a leafy street in a suburb where even Catholics were discreet about their faith, became home to twenty-four children speaking half a dozen European languages and as varied in national characteristics as Norwegians were from Italians.

Mrs. Goetz, now the wife of an Australian soldier (even if he did shoulder nothing more lethal than a pick) resigned and moved up to Yass, where Bertold drank beer, swore like an Aussie, and loaded wheat trucks while whistling Beethoven. Wielder of immense power as a corporal, he had under his command Private Willi Schlesinger who, despite the extremes of heat and cold, wore his complete uniform on all occasions.

A Mrs. Ivy Mackay, late of the Dr. Barnardo's Homes of Essex, England, and widowed by a German bomb, was appointed as matron of the Abraham Samuelson Memorial Home for Jewish Children, or as it quickly became known to the locals, the Jews' Home. It would be untrue to say that there was harmony and understanding between the Jewish children and their middle-class Protestant neighbors. Left to themselves, the children would have quickly been absorbed into the life of that small suburban community; prejudice on the part of the adult Christians and the Jewish fear of loss of identity made it almost impossible.

The division showed up in many curious ways. The Jews' Home, for example, would not shop locally. Their need to eat only kosher food meant that the local butcher could not supply them; the meat came twice a week on the train from a shop in Bondi. By the time it reached the pretty North Shore station, it oozed blood and was usually dumped by

77

irate station assistants in the station's bike shed to be fetched after school by Bill or me.

The Saturday Sabbath meant that we could not play in the street with the Gentile children. On Sundays, we would watch them either dressed up and walking to church or going on picnics with their families. At school the next day, they boasted of seeing goannas as big as crocodiles, snakes that could swallow a dog whole, and all this in a nature reserve a mile or so from the end of our street! Ruti would turn to me for verification of these tales of the indigenous wildlife. As an Australian, I was torn between rubbishing these outrageous claims and a nationalistic pride in a fauna of which I had no personal knowledge. On one occasion as we sat close together at the edge of the mansion's empty swimming pool, I told her of the huge man-eating sharks that swam off Bondi Beach, and of how I had actually once saved Solly from their massive jaws. I remained her hero only until after dinner that night, by which time Solly had told her, "Jake is pulling your leg, Ruti—it was *me* that saved *him*."

Her mother, now widowed in a strange land, visited her every Sunday, grayer than ever, worn out from a week's work in a factory and ready to collapse into a chair after the long walk from the station. She sewed army shirts for ten hours a day and showed Ruti her bank savings book. "Soon, you will leave here, my darling, and we shall have a flat together." I felt a knot of anxiety when Ruti told me this; any talk of us being parted filled me with morbid loneliness.

Ivy Mackay, who insisted on being addressed as Matron, took this as a sign of ill health and prescribed regular dosing with cod-liver oil. It was her universal panacea. Solly got it for failing to do his homework or his kitchen duties. Manfred actually liked the turgid stuff and grew even plumper on it, supplemented by nocturnal pantry raids and his mother's neverending supply of chocolates. Mitzi Strauss worked in a coffee shop in George Street, bustling around the hissing urns and flirting with the customers, almost exclusively Jewish refugees. They would arrive at the café shortly after ten in the morning, their briefcases bulging with documentary proof of their former European status, all of which meant less than nothing to potential Australian employers. They bowed and addressed each other as *Herr Doktor* and condemned the Australian legal, medical, and dental professions which insisted that they go back to university to obtain an Australian degree. Many of them worked a night shift in a munitions factory and bemoaned their ruined hands. Mitzi Strauss tut-tutted over them but secretly despised them.

Thanks to Uncle Siddy, there was no shortage of coffee, tea, and sugar in that café. He had taken to the black market like a duck to water. He and Mitzi Strauss were thick as thieves. Love and the need to make a quick quid drew them together, in business and in bed. Siddy could obtain anything that was scarce, from entire ration books to a tank of petrol; he knew which flats were about to become vacant and where American servicemen could trade cigarettes for liquor. Whatever you wanted in wartime Sydney, Siddy the Yid—as he was widely known to police and public alike—could get it for you.

As his reputation spread, Mrs. Pearlman asked him not to visit Solly and me in the Jews' Home. I think she disapproved of him as much for his liaison with Mitzi Strauss as for his illicit way of life. He compromised to the point where he drove Mitzi to the Home in his flash car, parked it outside, and sat in it smoking a cigar. He would send Mitzi in with a ten-shilling note each for Solly and me. Mrs. Mackay, cannier with money than any of her employers were presumed to be, opened post-office savings accounts for us. "Many a mickle makes a muckle," she quoted mysteriously.

I worried about Solly. Our four-year age gap had grown to an unbridgeable chasm. He was nearly eleven, tall, slim, with a mind like quicksilver and a tongue that would and could lash and beguile you in one breath. He slipped in and out of trouble effortlessly. Teachers wrote warning notes about him and then tore them up as he promised to reform. Ruti hated him. He stole her brassiere from the clothesline, stuffed his socks inside the cups, and strutted around the street with it on his chest.

He had completely eradicated all memories of our past life or at least locked them away, so that any attempts I made to remind him of it were met with a shrug. Uncle Siddy was his idol, and Manfred his constant coconspirator. Mitzi Strauss had virtually adopted him; she divided her gifts equally between Solly and Manfred. I was deeply shocked when she fell into the habit of referring to Manfred as her little mannikin.

"Don't you remember anything, Solly?" I pleaded. "What about how Carmel used to call us her little mannikins, then pissed off and left us with nothing but a bloody tin of plum jam?"

"Why do you keep going on with all that old stuff, Jake? Mitzi's a beaut woman—not a bit like Carmel."

"Well, she'd better not call me her little mannikin, that's all!"

Solly smiled a secret smile. He pulled back the curtains of the front room and beckoned me over. I could see Uncle Siddy, down in the street, slumped behind the wheel of a big black boxy car. Curls of cigar smoke rose in the air. A race guide rested on the steering wheel.

"Whaddya think about that, Jake?" Solly asked.

"It reminds me of the coppers' car when they took us away," I said miserably.

He turned on me angrily. "You'd turn cream sour, wouldn't you!"

He opened the window and yelled out, "G'day there, Uncle Siddy, got a good thing for the fourth at Randwick?"

Siddy waved back at him; Solly turned to me and smirked. "I'll let you into a secret, Jake—me and Manfred are going to live with Aunty Mitzi in a big house in Bondi!" He did a little jig for joy. "And that's not all—Uncle Siddy will be there too!"

I hit him, with the flat of my hand, right across the face.

He didn't cry out; he bit his lip and blinked back the tears. He walked in carefully controlled steps to the door, turned around, and said through clenched teeth, "I'm glad you're not coming with us."

The room grew dark as I sat on the edge of the bed. I took the *mezuzah* out of the bedside locker and unwrapped it. Its little eye stared coldly back at me. "And thou shalt bind them for a sign upon your doorposts," the Bible said. Well, it wouldn't be *our* doorpost, that's for sure, I told myself.

I needed to talk to somebody. I thought of Bill, that exponent of rational argument. No, I did not need his cold, objective solutions, always right like a key that fits only one door. I put the *mezuzah* back in my locker—it posed more problems than it answered. As the stinging of my hand from hitting Solly waned, so did the turmoil inside of me. Slowly I began to realize that what he had schemed for his future was no more or less than what I had wished as a future for Ruti and myself. He had achieved what I had only dreamed of. I was not angry or even concerned at the kind of life he would lead with Mitzi Strauss, Manfred, and Uncle Siddy. Worst of all, it did not distress me, as it should have, that he calmly assumed that we would be separated. No, I had hit him because his life now had direction, and mine had none.

As though through a lifting fog, I heard Siddy's car start up; there was a cheeky toot on the horn. I opened the window and leaned out. Mitzi was standing by the car door, alternately hugging Manfred and Solly.

"Next Sunday, little mannikins," she called out over the revving motor, "Mitzi will come for you, und den ve shall haff such fun altogezzer!" Reluctantly, she let the two boys go and climbed into the car. Siddy tooted again, let out the clutch, and the huge car shot off up the hill, leaving a pall of blue smoke hanging in the late afternoon air.

7

Mrs. Pearlman arrived at the Abraham Samuelson Memorial Home an hour or so before sunset on the following Friday. As she was not permitted to travel on the Sabbath, it was obvious that she would stay until it was concluded at sunset on Saturday. She wore a wide-brimmed hat and, in addition to her handbag, struggled with a briefcase quite at odds with her summery appearance. She marched up the steps to be met by Matron Ivy Mackay, who conducted her straight into her office. The door closed behind them, leaving the children to wonder why the woman who controlled their destinies should choose this inappropriate time to visit.

The Sabbath tables were already set. Candles had been lit, a glass of wine stood ready beside the sweet Sabbath loaf. Bill, as the eldest male present, would conduct the Sabbath eve service at the table. We stood behind our chairs in our usual places, waiting for Mrs. Mackay, to whom the Hebrew service was as incomprehensible as her Scottish brogue was to us. Solly and Manfred fidgeted and jostled each other. Bill waited impassively, the prayer book open on the table before him.

From across the table, I watched Ruti as she played mother to the smaller children. The death of her father had created both a bond and a barrier between us. She had pathetically few memorable days to recall of her life with her father. What events she did describe to me were invariably overcast by his constant illness. I would listen to Ruti's recital with barely concealed impatience, longing for the time when Henry Kahn would be replaced in her consciousness by Jacob Kaiser. Perhaps it was this recurring idea of my being a "father" to Ruti that kept in check my barely understood sexual longing for her. This, and the closeness of our little group in the Jews' Home, made overt feelings something to be avoided.

Ivy Mackay and Rosie Pearlman came into the dining room. Mrs. Pearlman took the reserved place beside Bill; Ivy Mackay went to another table and stood by her chair. Mrs. Pearlman tapped on a glass with a knife.

"I wish you all a good Sabbath," she began. "I have some announcements to make, but first Wolfgang will conduct the Sabbath service." She nodded to Bill, who seemed to grow in stature by being referred to by his true name.

"'And it was evening and it was morning—the sixth day,'" he intoned. "'And the heaven and the earth were finished and all their host. And on the seventh day God had finished His work which He had made; and He rested on the seventh day from all His work which He had made. And God blessed the seventh day, and He hallowed it . . .'"

The prayer went on to thank God for the deliverance from Egypt and for making Jews the eternal guardians of the Sabbath.

Bill pronounced the blessing for wine and for bread. Small pieces of the sweet loaf were broken off, sprinkled with salt, and passed around the tables. This simple ceremony made me feel as though I was part of a universal family—a family that even included shady dealers like Uncle Siddy.

Minny came in pushing a dinner wagon of steaming soup. Above the noise of serving and eating, Mrs. Pearlman said: "Now, there are lots of stories going around about what is to happen to some of you. Well, I can tell you that for some it is good news and for others—well, it could also be good news, depending upon how they take it."

Bill was smiling enigmatically; Solly and Manfred looked as though they would burst from pent-up excitement. Ruti looked down at her plate. I stared hard at her, willing her to look at me.

Mrs. Pearlman took a sheet of Abraham Samuelson Memorial Home notepaper from her briefcase, placed it on the table in front of her, then ignored it. "First, I wish to announce that Wolfgang's father has been discharged from the army. As a result, his son will now be able to leave here and once more live with his parents." She patted Bill on the back and continued.

"Solomon Kaiser—little Solly, as you all know him— has been, er, invited, shall we say"—she was picking her words carefully—"to reside with Mrs. Mitzi Strauss and Manfred." Mrs. Pearlman watched me as she spoke. Despite the rumors that had flown around the Jews' Home, fueled by Bill's silence, Manfred's sly looks, and Ruti's attempts to keep the conversation inconsequential, I knew our lives were going to change. It was only my own that was still without official direction.

"Our dear Ruti," Mrs. Pearlman was saying in a voice that seemed far away, "will also join her mother who now has her own flat—in Bondi, isn't it, Ruti?—and is now in charge of shirt production at the factory of our own treasurer, Mr. Joe Symonds."

Minny came back to collect the dishes. The silence was unbearable. I could only think of that earliest day at the Abraham Samuelson Memorial Home when I had lost my temper at the first intimation I had of losing Solly. I would not break down this time; let them all go their own bloody way, I'd survive without them. Bitterly, I searched for something to hate in all of them. Bill, for his apparent ability to ride out any storm; Solly, for his compliant nature; Ruti, for . . . for not setting up home with me on the shores of Bondi.

The girls left the table and went into the kitchen to collect the main course. Ruti reappeared through the swinging doors with the dishes. She served Mrs. Pearlman, and as she did so, a few words passed between them. Ruti approached me, placed my dinner in front of me, and as her hair brushed my ear, whispered, "She has good news for you too, Jacob."

It was too much to bear. Her nearness, the warmth of her voice, the smell of her freshly washed skin, the gentle curve of her breasts. For one moment, all I loved was so close. In that instant I forgot my bitterness at her leaving. I stood up, wrapped my arms clumsily around her, and said softly but fiercely, "I love you, Ruti."

I was almost fifteen. Ruti was sixteen. As we stood there, we were ageless, deaf, and blind, oblivious to the gasps, cheers, and handclaps. A marvelous, pervading warmth enveloped me. It was a feeling I had only known when I used to insinuate my body between the cracks of two giant rocks at North Bondi, and the reflected heat of the winter sun was a sensual experience I could not then understand. Now, with our arms about each other, I finally understood.

When the noise died down, Ivy Mackay, belatedly exerting her authority, said, "Well, I never! We can't have *that* sort of behavior. Leave the room, Jacob—at once."

Mrs. Pearlman stopped me. "It was beautiful, Jacob," she said for everyone to hear. "Don't worry, wait for me in Matron's office."

I left the door ajar. I could hear the children singing the

Grace After Meals. It was more like a jolly singsong than praying. My one contribution to the religious life of the children of the Abraham Samuelson Memorial Home was to persuade the reffo kids to sing the Grace to the tune of "Waltzing Matilda."

Its last notes died away as Mrs. Pearlman entered the office. She patted away the last crumbs from her lips and sat down, not behind the big desk but facing me, our knees almost touching.

"You are very fond of Ruti, aren't you?"

She obviously did not expect an answer but went on: "We are expecting many more children to arrive from Europe, Jacob. The few we can save are escaping from Germany through Switzerland. Australia is one of the last countries that will still accept refugees. The Home has to look after them. That is why we are pleased that Bill and Manfred and Ruti are leaving. We must have their places for the newcomers." She leaned forward and said, "So far as Solly is concerned—it was a difficult decision. He wanted so much to go with Manfred, and . . . and well, Jacob, we just could not find a family that could take both of you."

Minny brought in two cups of tea. I said, "You and I always seem to be drinking tea when my life is about to change."

"Oh, you remember that day when the police sergeant sent you to me?" Mrs. Pearlman took a notebook from her briefcase. Without raising her head, she said, "We, that is to say, the committee have decided that you should become an apprentice." Her voice became toneless and formal. "We have arranged with Grayson and Roberts of—"

"What's an apprentice?" I interrupted.

"Well, it's a young person who goes to work and is taught a trade."

"Ruti says she is going to university—does that mean she is more cleverer than me?" I spoke badly deliberately to emphasize my point.

Mrs. Pearlman, although childless, had learned enough of the tricks of children to know when she was being provoked. She ignored my bad grammar. "No, Jacob, it is what her parents wanted for her. And why her mother works so hard," she added. "Now, where was I? Ah yes, Grayson and Roberts of 188 Sussex Street in the city—they are printers and do all the work for the Home." She referred to her notebook. "You will become an apprentice printer. We have arranged for you to leave the home on Monday week, and you will board with Mrs. Rothfield at 22 Waverley Crescent, Bondi Junction."

Of all that stream of instruction Mrs. Pearlman had just issued, all that penetrated was the news that I would be moving to Bondi Junction, a short distance from where Ruti would be living. I could see her now—in her bathing suit, her body lying on the beach beside me, the sun coating that pale European skin. In the winter 1 would show her my secret places in the crevices of the rocks where the sun reached but the wind could not. I would walk with her to the top of the cliffs on the south headland where our father had labored—and died. But I would never ever show her the Balconies and its mean house-of-cards rooms.

"Wake up, Jacob!" Mrs. Pearlman was tapping me on the knee with her notebook.

I said, sullenly, "Is that the good news?"

She looked quite disconcerted; it was not what she had expected from the recipient of such charitable foresight. She asked me if I was worried about Solly, was I frightened to leave the Home, did the idea of going to work upset me? To all these questions, I shook my head. "Well," she said, "that's it then; you may go back and tell the others of your new start in life. And always remember, you owe it all to the Abraham Samuelson Memorial Home."

Perhaps Mrs. Pearlman was right about the debt. My apprenticeship as a printer's compositor awakened a creative streak in me that I had not known existed. I learned quickly and enjoyed reading the type in reverse and from right to left. The foreman was a wizened man in his sixties who addressed me variously as Jack, Jake, and occasionally as Ikey, especially when I made a mistake with the change after buying the journeymen's lunches. The employees were mainly old men called out of retirement to take the places of men who went to the war. At lunchtime they would scan the newspapers for the names of those missing in action.

I represented something inexplicable to them. They knew Jews as the businessmen who came into the printery and ordered work, as bookies whose pictures appeared on the sports pages, with names like Solomon and Eizenberg tagged to them. The workmen shopped at Danny's Bazaar in Bathurst Street. "I beat him down a quid on an overcoat," one boasted.

"How come you're not like them?" the machinist who operated the huge, noisy flatbed printing press asked me.

"Like what?" I asked nervously.

"Leave the kid alone," the foreman said. "What he means," he said kindly to me, "is he didn't expect to find a—"

"A Jew boy working and getting his hands dirty," I finished for him.

"Well, that and then there's those reffos coming here. All they seem to do is sit around and drink bloody coffee all day long."

If I was a puzzle to them, I was no less an enigma to my-self. The men's crude arguments had driven a wedge between myself and the Schlesingers, Mitzi Strauss, and even the Kahns. How many kinds of Jews were there? I longed for somebody to talk to. I felt as though I were entering a mine-field where I could be shattered by Jew and Gentile both.

That night at dinner, I said to Mrs. Rothfield, "What do you think of Gentiles?"

"*Dreck!*"

"What does that mean?"

"*Dreck!*" she repeated. "In Yiddish it means 'shit,' but a lady shouldn't say such a word."

"Why?"

"Because I'm a lady—ach, I see what you mean, Yakov. You haven't got eyes? You don't see them drunk on every corner? You don't see them beating their wives?"

"Have you seen them, Mrs. Rothfield?"

"Already he answers my question with a question! Eat, my boy, eat, and don't drink and don't go out with *shiksas!*"

That expression I knew from the days when Uncle Siddy swanned around with Gentile women. Mrs. Rothfield had, with this one word, discounted all non-Jewish women as being inferior—worse!—forbidden as was proscribed, non-kosher food.

Apart from Carmel, I had had very little contact with Gentile women; the ones I knew best were the three or four who worked in the bindery of the printery. They were invari-ably kind to me, offering me cakes that they had baked or a sandwich, lifting up a corner of it to assure me there was no ham in it. One of them, a gaunt woman with fiery eyes, in-cluded a religious tract from the Watch Tower Society with her gift of cake.

Much of the printing done by Grayson and Roberts was

for the many Masonic Lodges. The brochures included quotations from the Old Testament, which dealt in detail with the building of Solomon's Temple. The foreman assumed that I, as a Jew, must be an expert on the subject. All I could add to his store of knowledge was that a cubit was as long as a man's forearm, information I had gleaned with great difficulty from Mr. Klapper when discussing the size of Noah's Ark.

Outside the printery, I led a solitary life with only the vitriolic tongue of Mrs. Rothfield to contend with. My meager wage went to pay my board and left me with a few shillings a week. I joined a local penny lending library but soon tired of the shelves filled with romance and detective novels. One day, as I walked down George Street in my short lunch break, I discovered the Sydney Municipal Lending Library. It occupied the upper floors of a huge wine cellar. The combined smell of fermenting wine and musty books was enough to entice me inside. Once there, I was lost in the tall stacks, where men in overalls like myself were selecting books. The classifications seemed endless—fiction, classics, history, politics, religion—and I did not know what to choose.

A man in a coverall was watching me. After a while, he came up and said, "A young fella like you should be reading about the struggle of the working classes." He propelled me along the aisle then stopped and took down a book. "You need this, comrade, and you'll understand about the great class struggle."

It was Robert Tressell's *The Ragged Trousered Philanthropists.*

The story concerned a bunch of housepainters, plumbers, and carpenters who worked somewhere in England and were always grumbling about their hard life and poor pay. It must have been about 1912 or so. The building firm that employed them was crook, the work was done on the cheap, and the men were usually sacked at the end of the job.

The story was unremittingly gloomy. The central character was a painter named Frank Owen, who when I later became more politically aware, I recognized as being an anarchist. But now, as I read the book, it aroused a mass of confusing thoughts in me. For one thing, Frank Owen was antireligious, or, more specifically, against Christianity, at whose door he laid all the blame for social inequity. Fat, pompous parsons were forever telling the workers to "know their place in life." They sided with the employers, preaching the "dignity of labor" to men who more often than not had no job anyway. The workers, who even at my young age, struck me as a spineless, whining lot, accepted their misery and ridiculed Frank Owen.

The book bore no relationship to me or the people I worked with at Grayson and Roberts. My workmates were well paid; they were skilled tradesmen who had money to bet on the races, take their families on picnics, and go once a week to the pictures. And they all belonged to a union. I was careful not to be seen reading it at the printery.

Tressell called his workmen ragged trousered philanthropists because they "quietly submitted like so many cattle to their miserable slavery for the benefit of others, but defended it and opposed and ridiculed any suggestions for reform." The book was sprinkled with lines such as . . . "Mother, how many more days do you think we'll have only dry bread and tea?" Well, Solly and I had been better off—we at least had plum jam to spread on ours!

My head was now stuffed with newly acquired, half-understood expressions such as Capital and Labor, Socialism, Private Ownership of Property, Shared Wealth, and Strength

Through Unity. I rolled these terms around on my tongue, waiting for a chance to use them. As we sat in the lunch-room at the printery, I listened to the men's conversation. It was very disappointing. If they were not preoccupied with the war, the talk was of the weekend's sport or the weather. If they told a joke, I was sent out on some spurious errand. The leading machinist, I discovered, was also the printing union representative. I could not join because I was an apprentice. I took false courage in speaking to him because his name was Frank, the same as the hero of *The Ragged Trousered Philanthropists.*

"Are you a socialist, Mr. Williams?" I asked him.

"Is the Pope a Jew, son?"

"I don't think so, Mr. Williams."

"Right, and I'm no bloody socialist either, Ikey."

"Why? I mean, I've been reading this book, and it says that all the workers in the world should unite and share—"

"Oh yeah, says who? Look, I've got this nice little home in Marrickville that used to be me mother's before she passed on, and you're trying to tell me that I should share it with any bugger that calls himself a bloody socialist!"

He calmed down, patted me on the shoulder, and told me that when I was old enough I should vote for the Labor Party "and keep your trap shut about socialism, Ikey. I'm not saying you had anything to do with it, but it's an International Jewish Plot!"

I was not game enough to remind him that in this printery, which thrived on Masonic work, he had also condemned Catholicism as an international plot.

In desperation, I turned to Mrs. Rothfield, notwithstanding her demonstrable passionate prejudices. Nervously I asked her if she knew what socialism was. She pointed to a picture on her mantelpiece of a youngish man in working clothes, leaning on a shovel. I asked her who it was.

"Who else?" she replied with a shrug. "My husband— may he rest in peace." I had not associated Mrs. Rothfield with a man who did physical work.

"Was he like my father? I mean, did he have to do that sort of work because of the Depression?" I asked. "Or was it because he was a socialist?"

"Oy, Yakov, you don't know much about anything, do you? What did they teach you in the Home? Only how to pray like a Yid? Nothing about your history?"

She took the photo down and propped it up against a vase. From the sideboard, she produced a photograph album. Sepia pictures showed a stony landscape and, in the far distance, a valley with tall trees. In some of the pictures, men with rifles slung over their backs labored alongside women; men in Arab headdress sat on horseback and watched.

Mrs. Rothfield's stubby finger pointed out her husband to me. "And that's me beside him," she said triumphantly. "I too was a socialist. We lived together on a kibbutz in Palestine. For fifteen years, we sweated it out there, battling Arabs, mosquitoes, the British, Turks—it was never-ending."

As she turned the pages, tents gave way to stone huts, rows of fruit trees appeared, and I could see children playing. I still had no idea what this had to do with socialism.

She shook her head in wonderment at my ignorance, putting it down to Australia being so far away from the things that were important in life. "Look, Yakov, a kibbutz is a collective farm where everyone is equal and everyone gets an equal share of what the farm produces. The trouble, my boy, was that the people who made up the kibbutz—in Australia you wouldn't hire them. They knew nothing about farms. Like my husband and me—we came from Warsaw, a big city, bigger than Sydney. Oh, we were socialists all right, straight out of the book!"

She snapped the album shut. "*Nu,* Yakov, what else do you want to know about socialism?"

In my quest for knowledge about socialism, the tally was one in favor (Frank Owen) and two against (Frank Williams and Mrs. Rothfield). I decided if I were to become a socialist, I would neither work on a farm like the late Mr. Rothfield nor be like poor Frank Owen who died of consumption, ground down by rapacious English landlords. There had to be a more congenial way to become a socialist; the Municipal Library had been the vehicle which had brought me this far; perhaps it would take me the next step along the way.

My search was temporarily interrupted by the printery enrolling me at the technical college to learn more of my trade. I became immersed in the world of the typographer and engraver, the papermaker and the ink-maker. Caslon and Plantin, Caxton and Mergenthaler were milestones not only in the history of printing but in my own wish to learn of the present by studying the past.

When the term at the technical college ended, I went back to the Municipal Library. I had not taken out another book since returning *The Ragged Trousered Philanthropists.* It had been classified under Fiction; I found a section headed Social, but it dealt with customs and had books that showed beautiful bare-breasted native women carrying jugs and baskets of fruit on their heads. Not one of them bore any resemblance to Mrs. Rothfield's pictures of herself as a young woman.

At the inquiry desk, I asked about books on socialism. A woman scribbled down some numbers and pointed vaguely toward the window. The intricacies of the Dewey Catalogue System were quite beyond me. Disheartened, I returned to the counter and found various leaflets advertising public meetings for Soroptimists, Theosophists, Unitarians, Fabianists, and Communists. Most of the meetings took place on Sundays in the Sydney Domain, a place the men at the printery had told me was full of metho-drinking derelicts. As I moved away from the counter, the woman beckoned to me. She took in my overalls and ink-stained fingers.

"Would you like to go to an interesting meeting, with young people of your own age?" she asked.

I nodded. She reached under the counter and gave me a leaflet, poorly printed in red ink on cheap paper.

"It's not far from here—just down Market Street, near the wharves. It's called the Eureka Youth League."

"What's it about?"

She folded the leaflet up quickly and told me to put it in my pocket. "Read it when you get home, sonny," she said conspiratorially and dismissed me from her mind.

I showed it that night to Mrs. Rothfield.

"Dreck!"

"Why?"

"Communists, you *schlemiel*," she yelled. "Not in my house, thank you very much!"

"Where does it say *communist!* All it says is that they are showing a film on Russian agriculture and"—I ran my finger down the type—"how the collective brings in the harvest in the Ukraine. Isn't that what you used to do in Palestine —the collective—the kibbutz?"

Mrs. Rothfield shook her head; she popped a sugar cube into her mouth and drank a glass of lemon tea with the spoon still in it. She peered at me over the top of the glass. "Yakov, my boy, from my mouth to God's ear. Let me tell you: We were socialists. They"—she stabbed the leaflet— "they are Communists, no better than the Cossacks who murdered us in Russia."

I felt tears of frustration filling my eyes. Whichever way I turned, I met with bigotry of one kind or another. Mrs. Rothfield hated the Gentiles and the Communists; Frank Williams hated socialists and Catholics and the International Jewish Conspiracy. In my little world bounded by Bondi and the Sussex Street printery, there was enough hatred and conflict to stoke a thousand consuming fires. I wanted to withdraw from it all. The safest place I knew was the deep crevices in the rocks at North Bondi, where only the warming sun could get me and the bitter winds of prejudice could never reach me. A place I would only share with Ruti.

8

I was a little ashamed that my thoughts had turned to Ruti
only at a time of confusion and self-doubt. In the first few
months of my apprenticeship, with its unaccustomed long
working hours and so many new things to learn and remember, I would collapse into bed at the end of the day, exhausted. Mrs. Rothfield taught me to play gin rummy and
how to eat the claggy dish called *cholent* without actually
gagging on it.

I had started work toward the end of summer. The winter
months seemed interminable, punctuated only by excitement
at new things learned in my trade. The smell of ink, the
thrashing noise of the presses, the lines of type that grew
under my hand—listening to the conversation of grown men
—my head could contain no more at one time than all this.
And yet I knew I needed company, someone of my own age.

As if in defiance of the prevailing morality that frowned
upon meetings other than those ordained by religious groups,
the Eureka Youth League met on a Sunday afternoon. In a
firetrap of a building, a dozen boys and girls in their early
and mid-teens sat on the floor in front of a single-cone radiator. The boys seemed to be wearing the clothes they went to
work in. Everyone had a red-and-black enamel hammer-and-

sickle badge. I had come dressed in my best clothes. (I realized too late that Mrs. Rothfield had tricked me into this to cause me the maximum embarrassment.)

I was introduced to them as Comrade Kaiser.

Everybody was comrade this and comrade that. There were Greek and Italian names sprinkled in among the ordinary Australian ones. I was asked politely whether I was of German descent, "like the Kaiser."

"By golly, no," I protested, "my name was pronounced *Kay-ser!*"

"All men are created equal," one of them said to me.

A chorus went up: "And are everywhere in chains!"

Cheered by this newfound egalitarianism, I said, "Well, I'm Jewish, y' know."

A deep voice from the back said, "Religion is a crutch for the masses."

Another chorus: "Karl Marx!"

A girl sitting next to me then asked me if I was a Trotskyist. And so it went, throughout the afternoon. My head was spinning with a new glossary of strange terms—anarchist, Bolshevik, Menshevik, deviationist, Stalinist, capitalist. I learned to say "Workers of the World, Unite. You Have Nothing to Lose but Your Chains" with something approaching conviction.

They wanted to know, too, if I was persecuted at work for my beliefs. I responded to their interest by telling them that now and again I was called Ikey.

"No, no, comrade," they chorused. "Is it because you are a Communist?"

The meeting broke up shortly after four o'clock. We were given bundles of leaflets to stick up on telegraph poles.

"You must fulfill your Stakhanovite norm, comrade," I was told.

"What is that?"

"The brave workers of the Soviet Socialist Republics must produce their quota for the State."

I had twenty-five posters to stick up—that was my quota. I was given a badge, assured I would make a good comrade, and let out into the pale wintry sunshine. The meeting had been grim, impersonal, dedicated, and humorless. I was not so sure that I would make a worthy member of the "lumpen proletariat." Besides, when I had asked an earnest-looking girl whether she had read *The Ragged Trousered Philanthropists*, she dismissed it as "typical of the weak-kneed English working classes." We parted at the corner of Market and George Streets. I never went back.

Once again, I felt alone and drifting. I dumped the leaflets in the gutter and pushed them down the drain with my foot. George Street on a Sunday afternoon was no place to try to find one's self. In either direction, it stretched out from the bridge to Central Railway, deserted and silent. A few dejected soldiers wandered aimlessly in search of girls, a fight, or a drink. Had they looked more carefully, they might have discovered Mitzi Strauss frothing up Vienna coffee and slicing up cheesecake for equally lonely German Jewish refugees.

Against my will, I started to walk in the direction of the Vienna Wald; there, I would get news of Solly and perhaps Uncle Siddy. I had only seen Solly a few times since we left the Abraham Samuelson Memorial Home. He had put on weight. He spoke to me with a cunning beyond his years and always had money in his pocket. Even in wartime Sydney, Mitzi Strauss had been able to get a telephone connected. From it, Uncle Siddy conducted his SP betting business, and Manfred and Solly were his runners.

The last occasion I saw Solly, I could hardly get him to stand still long enough to speak to him. He fidgeted; he wasn't interested in what I was doing, and it was useless to try to impress him with the pittance of a wage that I earned. He airily mentioned names that I sometimes caught sight of in the Sunday tabloid press. They were Siddy's black-market booze and cigarette customers. It was clear Solly was moving in a very different world from mine, and I was in danger of severing the small contact I had with him if I criticized his way of life.

I had only gone a few yards when I saw a gathering of young people all wearing what appeared to be some sort of uniform. The boys had on navy blue pants and light blue shirts with scout-type scarves; the girls were dressed the same, only they wore skirts. They were talking loudly, and there was much laughter. As I drew near, they entered a doorway between two shops. I hurried toward them and reached them just as the last few were entering. A girl looked up and down the street, then called out, "We're all here now. I'll close the door."

It was Ruti. Still shepherding people around, I thought absurdly; still being the little mother. I ran up, calling her name just as she slipped behind the steel grille door.

"Jacob, oh Jacob, I've thought so much about you. How are you, where have you been, where are you living?" She pressed her body against the grille, making crisscross patterns on her chest. I put my hand through and took hers.

"God, Ruti," I said, "can you get this thing open?"

She slid the grille back, nearly jamming our hands in it. A voice called out from up the stairs. "Hurry up, Ruti! The meeting is about to start."

My heart sank. "What meeting, Ruti? Why are you dressed like that?"

She dragged me inside and shut the grille again. I put my arms around her. She did not resist but neither did she return my warmth. In the darkness of the doorway, I tried to kiss her. She said gently, "You never came to see me, Jacob." She pulled away from me and led me up the stairs.

"Where are you taking me, Ruti?"

"To our meeting."

"Not another one," I said dejectedly.

"What do you mean—not another one? You've never been here before, have you?"

"Skip it," I replied. "You lead and I'll follow. Just tell me: What is that uniform you're wearing?"

She said, over her shoulder and a little out of breath, "It's called *Habonim*— it means 'The Builders,' in Hebrew."

"Ruti," I begged, "it's a lovely afternoon. Won't you come for a walk with me? We could go to the Gardens and talk."

"Oh no, Jacob, this is very important. It's all about our future in Palestine. Yours and mine," she added hastily.

As we entered the room, I had a quick mental picture of Ruti scrabbling in the earth like the Rothfields, with me standing guard over her with a rifle.

The first person I saw was Bill. He was seated in the room with a semicircle of boys and girls around him. He nodded recognition as though it was the most natural thing in the world that I should be there. Ruti pulled me down on the floor beside her. I noticed everyone was wearing a pin-on badge that had the Star of David on it. Behind Bill, a huge flag with the same emblem hung on the wall. His voice had deepened since I had last seen him; there was a faint patina of reddish whiskers on his chin. He was talking about camps that had been planned to fit in with everyone's study. I looked at Ruti. She was taking notes in that same spiky German handwriting I knew so well.

"You will all take your Hebrew grammar with you and your extracts of Herzl's speeches to the Vienna Zionist Congress," Bill said.

He looked over all the heads directly at me. "What about you, Jacob?"

"Oh, I shall take Robert Tressell's *The Ragged Trousered Philanthropists*," I said sarcastically.

"I do not know such a book," he replied calmly.

"What about Karl Marx's *Das Kapital* then, Bill?"

"You are studying economics?" he replied with the nearest he could come to sarcasm.

I stood up. "No, Wolfgang, I'm just a poor bloody worker."

There was a scattering of nervous laughter. Ruti was tugging at my coat. Bill held up his hand for silence. "Our national home also requires workers," he said quietly. "It could not exist if all its citizens were students."

Ruti whispered, "What is the matter with you, Jacob? It is not like you to be rude."

I gripped her hand fiercely. I tried to explain my inner conflict to her—how I had just come from a meeting of young Communists who wanted to destroy the world then rebuild it, who preached a doctrine of equality I could not comprehend. And now, here I was trying to grapple with another philosophy of rebuilding a desolate country that I only knew as a Biblical dream.

"It takes time, Jacob, to sort out one's feelings and beliefs," she said. "It is not only you who has such a problem. What about all those kids who came from overseas to Australia? A place they could not even point to on a map. And what about their parents? Reffos, they're called, from now until the day they die." She stopped suddenly, realizing what she had said. "At least you were lucky enough to be born here," she finished lamely.

Someone was winding up a portable gramophone. Strange Middle Eastern music blared out. Boys and girls formed a ring and began to dance to it. Ruti grabbed me by the arm and pushed me into the ring. In spite of myself, I found my feet following the gyrations of those around me. The rhythm was infectious, kids were singing to the music, and I was a part of it all. When it stopped, we were all out of breath and laughing together. Except Bill. He was still sitting down, writing furiously, oblivious to everything that went on around him.

Ruti, her cheeks flushed, started a round of introductions. Without exception, everyone I met was from some part or other of Europe. I was the only Australian-born kid there. And we were all Jews.

I had a lot to learn about the world, about this new Australia, about Jewish society and where I fit in. I would help Ruti and she would help me. That is the way I hoped it would be—only time would tell. But when the meeting was over, she did not leave with me. She went off with the Habonim group to one of their member's homes. I was not invited.

The only life to be found in Sydney on a late Sunday afternoon was down at Circular Quay. The ferries would be returning from Manly and the zoo with families tired and cross after a day's outing. Or lovers would leave the Middle Harbor ferry arm-in-arm, their hair awry, their cheeks glowing from the wind as they hung over the ferry side. The Quay would smell of diesel oil and fish and chips. As the families left the boats, they would run the gauntlet of tired men selling cotton candy and pinwheels. Fathers would fumble in their pockets, make a quick calculation for fares home, then buy from them to placate a grizzling child.

I was still wearing my bar mitzvah suit, now unbearably tight. I could not close the coat against the encroaching cold wind that whistled up George Street as though it were being forced through a funnel. I walked toward the Quay, on the opposite side of the street to Mitzi's Vienna Wald café. At the water's edge, by the grimy green railing, I stared at my distorted reflection. It was covered in the detritus that eddied around the pylons.

"You'd think people would be a bit more careful where they threw their rubbish, wouldn't you?"

I looked up. It was the girl from the Eureka Youth League, the one with glasses who had scorned my reference to *The Ragged Trousered Philanthropists*. She was hanging over the railing beside me.

"I've just come from Manly," she said. She pointed to the berthed ferry. "I saw you from the top deck. You looked like a wet week, so I thought I'd come over and cheer you up." She linked her arm through mine. "We workers have got to look after each other," she said, laughing.

With her beside me, I immediately felt at one with the crowds that were crossing the road to the tramcars. A child who had a moment before seemed to me a snotty little beast was now simply an accepted member of a loving family. We didn't walk so much as saunter among the home-goers, content to be swept along in the gathering dusk.

"Which way are you going, Jack?" She laughed again. "See, I remember your name. I'll bet you don't remember mine. No, of course you don't. It's Peg or Peggy, if you like. Peggy Piper. And your second name is Kaiser. That makes P.K. like the chewing gum. I reckon I'll have to stick to you, Jack!"

The tramcars were lined up; conductors were changing the destination boards: Botany Bay, La Perouse, Maroubra, Bellevue Hill, Bondi.

Peg said, "Take your pick, Jack. Tuppence to Bondi, fourpence to La Perouse, we'll go Dutch."

105

"Where do you want to go, Peg? Point Piper, where the nobs live? Is that where the ancestral home is?"

"Nope, I've got a little room in Darlinghurst. But I bet you live in Bondi, where all the Jews hang out."

I swung around and looked at her. Behind her glasses, her eyes shone without malice. Her lips were still parted in a smile. The anger died in me. Still, I felt I had to fight back for the real or imagined insult.

"Some pretty crook girls live in Darlo," I said.

"It's you blokes that make 'em like that," she came back at me.

I thought of Uncle Siddy and his boasting about the "pros" he knew and the *shiksas* he had flaunted in front of our father. And here I was, on a Sunday afternoon at Circular Quay with a *shiksa*, a Gentile girl hanging on my arm. Was I in danger of following in his footsteps? A little thrill went through me. I pulled Peg closer to me and said, "Let's go to Darlo. We can get a cuppa tea at the Cross."

"Oh, Mister Big Spender, eh? You sure you're not related to Eizenberg the bookie?"

There it was again. The Ikey jokes that I could never get away from. "Hell, Peg," I gritted, "can't you ever stop picking on us?"

She took off her glasses and wiped them carefully on her jumper. "Do you believe in equality, Jack?" she asked. "That all men are created equal, that—"

"Is that straight out of your Eureka Youth League Handbook, Peg?"

She laughed out loud. "Strewth, Jack, is that how it sounded?"

I laughed with her. "Come on, Peg, if you want to play at being equal, I'll pay the tram fares, and you can make me a cup of tea."

As the tram trundled up William Street, she told me she was a pantry maid at Sydney Hospital. She hoped to become a nurse as soon as she was old enough. Her family came from Bathurst.

"We live only a few doors from Ben Chifley, the Labor member of Parliament," she said proudly. "My dad was a shunter in the railway yards before he got hurt." She rummaged in her handbag. I told her I was paying the fares. "Don't get upset, Jack," she said. "I'm only looking for a cigarette."

I was astounded. She pulled out a packet of Cavaliers, five for threepence, and lit up. A man opposite me winked. I blushed and looked out at the rain sweeping over Woolloomooloo. Peg puffed away and, as the tram reached the top of the hill, she flipped the butt away and said, "Righto, Jack, we get off here, and then it's a short trot down past the fire station."

We ran hand-in-hand down the road, the rain cutting into us. Just past the fire station, Peg pulled up. She pointed down the road.

"That's the Jews' Hall down there, isn't it, Jack?"

It certainly was—the very place where the taxi driver had dropped Solly and me and where we first met Mrs. Rosie Pearlman what seemed a lifetime ago.

"Oh well," she said cheerily, "they never did me any harm, not like some of the other dirty buggers that hang around here." She took out a key. "Here we are—Peg's Palace! I hope I've got a deener for the gas-ring." She steered me up a flight of stairs, took another key, and opened the door. "In you go, Jack. I'll only be a minute. I've got to go to the lav first."

I switched on the light. Far off, I could hear the gurgle of a cistern. The first thing I did was to pull down the blind because of the wartime blackout regulations. Peg (or some previous tenant) had painted a funny face on the blind. If it had not been for that, I would have felt as though I had stepped back in time to the first days when our family had moved to the Balconies. The room had the same atmosphere of tawdry cheapness, of transitory living, of impermanence, of people who had moved through it and each had left a small part of a life behind.

I found the gas meter and fed a shilling into it. Not having matches, I could not light the tiny fire or the gas-ring. A bed in the corner was covered with a quilt bearing a Sydney Hospital emblem; so did the towel thrown across the end. The rest of the furniture had surely come from the secondhand shops along Oxford Street.

Peg had stuck Eureka Youth League posters on the flaky walls and, incongruously, a picture of a Clydesdale draft horse standing proudly in a paddock. I looked in a cupboard for tea and milk.

"Right there, Jack, in the canister. You'll have to have condensed milk, though." Peg was locking the door. "Keep the nosy parkers out, eh?"

"I put a shilling in the meter, Peg, but I haven't any matches."

"That was my part of the treat," she said. She lit the gas-ring and the fire. "Let's make toast. I've got bread and butter and plum jam."

"I'll skip the plum jam, thanks."

She put a little cloth on the table, explaining that her mother had given it to her when she left home. I had taken off my restricting suit coat and kicked off my wet shoes. Peg had also removed her sweater and shoes. She was wearing a man's check shirt and a skirt of knobbly tweed. She had taken out the comb, and her hair now hung down her back.

108

The little gas fire hissed and spluttered but did not go out. We drank our tea and munched on arrowroot biscuits with unreal decorum, attentive to each other's needs beyond the bounds of required politeness.

It was obvious we were both nervously dragging out this little ceremony, frightened of what might ensue once it was over. Peg removed and replaced her glasses half a dozen times and chattered away about her childhood in Bathurst. I talked of the day-to-day happenings at the printery. I don't think we listened to half of what the other was saying. When the last cup of tea was drunk and the last biscuit gone, Peg said, "I thought I had another shilling for the meter, but I haven't. It's going to get darn cold, Jack."

We both looked accusingly at the gas fire. Peg said, "In Bathurst, we used to nick the coal from the railway yard."

The fire gave a pathetic pop and went out. I made a silly joke. "Well, I've paid the piper, now you can call the tune!"

"You ought to be on the stage like that Yid comedian, whatsisname, Mo."

Before I could reply, Peg got up and kissed me on the lips.

It was a soft kiss, almost a brushing of the lips; her eyes were open, and I looked into them. They were blue, with tiny flecks of gold like the palest opal. I could also see the lightly tanned and freckled V of her neckline and the embroidered top edge of her brassiere.

She left me and turned out the light. The heating elements of the gas fire still glowed faintly in the dark. I heard the rustle of clothing and a hard sound as her belt fell to the floor. She moved across the window and released the blind, which went up with an angry snap. Now the room was suffused with streaky light. Peg was standing by the bed in her underwear.

"Well, come on, you ninny, don't sit there all by yourself," she said. "Let's snuggle up and keep warm." She turned the Sydney Hospital cover down neatly, then pulled back the blankets. She gave a little shudder of cold and got into bed.

I stood up. "You've still got your socks on, Peg," I said inanely.

"You can keep yours on too, Jack, but you'd better take those wet trousers off."

I went across to the darkest corner of the room and took my pants off. The deep brown eyes of the Clydesdale horse seemed to reassure me—against what, I did not know. I took off my shirt and stood shivering with cold and fright. It seemed miles from where I stood to where Peg lay under the blankets with just her head showing.

"The working class can kiss my arse, here we're snug in bed at last!" she sang to the tune of "O Tannenbaum."

I measured the distance to the bed, put my head down, and ran across the room, knocking over a chair as I went. Peg had the blankets back, and I hopped in. I lay beside her, rigid and unyielding. My heart was banging away and did not quiet down until the warmth of our bodies fused and my breathing steadied enough for me to speak.

An ambulance with siren blaring was halted in the traffic right outside the window. We heard a voice calling to someone to "Get out of the way, yer mug!"

Peg, lying on her back, said, "Another one for St. Vinny's. I hear 'em all night long." She propped herself up on her elbow and looked at me. "Well, I'll be blowed, Jack. You haven't got a Jewish nose."

"How many Jews do you know, Peg?"

"Well, there's Doctor Isaacs in Casualty. A really nice bloke. He gave me some pills for my hay fever. And then there's—"

"Okay, that makes two—one has and one hasn't. So you're only half-right, aren't you?"

"Oh, what does it matter anyway, Jack. Come to think of it, my uncle in Bathurst has a big nose, but I reckon that's the booze."

Peg turned toward me. The hard wiring of her brassiere poked into my chest. I moved away. I also had a problem that I pretended Peg had not noticed. She stroked my forehead.

"You're really only a kid, Jack," she said softly. "Don't take any notice of me. When you're raised in the country and you come from a big family, well, you sort of learn about—things." She sat up and thumped the pillows then lay down again on her side with her back to me. "I tell you what, we'll lie like spoons—you cuddle up to me, and I'll bet before you can say 'antidisestablishmentarianism' we'll be sound asleep."

As far as Peg herself was concerned, she was right. I listened to her even breathing and tried to make pictures out of the cracks in the ceiling plaster. I saw the Murray River and its tributaries and named them over and over until my erection subsided, then I sneaked out of the bed. Peg never moved. I dressed, except for my soggy shoes, and let myself out of the room. I had no idea of the time. I sat on the stairs and put my shoes on, snapping the rotten laces. Outside the rain had stopped, but the wind, now clean and sharp, was at my back as I started to walk from Darlinghurst to Bondi Junction. When I reached Oxford Street, I could see the face of the Paddington Town Hall clock. It was a few minutes after midnight.

There were two long and lonely stretches on that walk. The first was alongside the high wall of the army barracks. Soldiers were asleep inside there, each in his own single cot

111

without the comforting warmth of a Peg Piper. I hugged myself with smug satisfaction at the thought of it.

Next, up past the Town Hall, past the hundreds of darkened shop fronts until the road widened at the first corner of Centennial Park. Through the railings, I could see the classic statuary, white, cold, and nude on sandstone plinths.

I called out loud to them.

"Hullo Ruti, hullo Peg, hullo Ruti, hullo Peg, hullo . . . hullo . . . hullo." Until I had passed them all.

9

As if it were not enough that it was winter, Bondi Beach was festooned with barbed wire. The army had laid coils of it from one end to the other. The wire was the official response to an imminent Japanese invasion, the forerunner of which was a Japanese submarine mother ship said to be cruising off the coast. It lobbed a dud shell right in the heart of the Bondi shopping center. There was panic among the Jewish community, many of whom had fled there from Europe. Some of them removed their entire households to the comparative safety of the North Shore, perhaps in the belief that Japanese invaders would not attempt to cross the Sydney Harbor Bridge.

Good-time girls took over the empty flats and entertained American soldiers. For a shilling or two, I showed the Americans how they could get access to the beach by following me on a zigzag path through the barbed wire.

With the money I earned from this and other small enterprises, such as filling discarded whisky bottles with cold tea or ginger ale, I was able to buy the cheap books in the Everyman Library series. On those cold, crisp, and sunny wintry Sunday afternoons, I would wedge myself into my secret place in the rocks and read.

I devoured Conan Doyle, R. L. Stevenson (too long-winded), R. M. Ballantyne, Mark Twain (envious of Tom for having a mate like Huck), and Henry Lawson, whose working men showed a lot more guts than the toadies in *The Ragged Trousered Philanthropists*. I read while traveling to and from work on the tram, and I read during meal breaks at the printery. The men said, "You'd read the label off a jam tin, wouldn't ya, Ikey?"

I read my way right through the winter. Mrs. Rothfield saw my light on late at night and decided that too much reading would ruin my eyes. She ordered me to switch the light off at half past nine. I bought a battery-powered bicycle torch and read under the blankets. When spring came, at last, I had acquired the detection skills of Sherlock Holmes, the survival ingenuity of Robinson Crusoe, and the egalitarianism of Henry Lawson's characters.

None of their qualities was applicable to my predicament as a sixteen-year-old Jewish boy in wartime Bondi. They did not assuage my desire for compatible company. What was worse, I did not know with whom I was compatible. Ruti had held out a hand then withdrawn it; Peg had offered herself with disarming honesty, and I had rejected her. In my heart, I knew my failings all too well; I had the capacity to love but lacked the courage to show it. I was afraid of being hurt. At work, I was morose, unable to respond to rough kindness, and all too ready to react to real or imagined slights.

I pinned all my hopes for happier times on the arrival of summer. It became an obsession with me. I bought a thermometer; my spirits rose and fell with the mercury. I told myself once it stayed over seventy degrees for three consecutive days, things would get better. Until then, I would go on reading, transplanting myself into unattainable situations, and, of course, nurturing my discontent as the only reality in my life.

Mrs. Rothfield bought me tins of Cornwall's Malt Extract. On the label was a chubby, napkinned baby holding aloft a huge iron girder. She assured me it would improve me all over. "Even the mind, Jacob; the brain needs feeding too." I agreed to eat the treacly stuff only until the day when the temperature reached seventy degrees.

By the end of October, it happened. Three glorious days on end dawned with cloudless skies and a warming westerly breeze that wrapped me in its folds. Early on the first Sunday morning following *my* official first days of summer, I took all the books and tied them in a bundle. With only the whirling sea birds as witnesses, I stood on the sheerest part of the cliff walk my father had helped to build and hurled them into the sea.

Looking to the north, I could see the sparkling crescent of Bondi Beach. The barbed wire reminded me of the religious pictures of Jesus with a crown of thorns pressed down on his forehead.

"Filthy bastards!" I screamed into the wind. "Stinking, rotten wire, I hate you, I hate you!"

I ran down the cliff path, climbed through the railing, and thrust the harsh gorse bushes aside until I felt the sand beneath my feet. I tore my clothes off and rushed into the sea where rocks and giant kelp weed broke the surface of the water. The waves beat me against the rocks, the blood ran down my body only to be wiped away in the next instant by the kelp fronds. A dog was tearing up and down the beach at the water's edge; its demented, frenzied bark reached out to me over the roar of the wind and the waves. I dived beneath the waves, down to the bottom where the kelp was rooted in the sand. I thought this was how I could see what it was like to drown. It could be a test of my courage too, and if I changed my mind, nobody but myself would ever know. I stayed until my lungs exploded, then shot to the surface. The dog was paddling frantically through the surf toward me.

"Go back, go back," I called. "Leave me alone!" It swam on strongly, its tail streaming out behind like the sweep oar of some strange miniature surfboat. As the dog reached me, I tore off a frond of the kelp and lashed at it.

The dog circled me, its eyes flecked with white. "You poor bugger," I relented, "you're scared stiff. Here boy, come on, let's get back to the beach."

I surfed into the shore and lay exhausted. The dog made it seconds later, shook itself, and dropped down beside me, sides heaving. With its head between its paws, it watched me dress, its tail giving a sporadic wave.

"Mrs. Rothfield doesn't like dogs," I told it, "and what's more, I bet you're not even Jewish." I gave it a farewell pat and set off up the beach through the barbed wire. When I reached the promenade and looked back, the dog was still lying on the sand.

I had never set foot in the Vienna Wald café. The windows onto George Street had half-height lacy curtains on brass rods; the door was fully curtained and always closed by means of a pneumatic spring. An extractor fan above the door blew delicious coffee fumes onto the street. The only way to see inside was to wait until someone entered and get a quick glimpse before the door shut behind them. I had done this a few times.

Now, on this mild Sunday afternoon, George Street did not look nearly so depressing; the clothing stores were showing off spring fashions. Soldiers, just returned from the Middle East, looked tanned and fit. Girls clung to them and begged to be taken to Luna Park. Vienna Wald was not the sort of café they would ever dream of entering; they knew instinctively that it was not for them. Down by the Quay, they could get a cup of tea and a buttered bun served by a perky girl in black with a lace-edged apron and a cap to match.

I stood at the curbside and watched them pause for a second or two; they sniffed the coffee aroma. A soldier might say, "Dunno how they drink that stuff—must be them reffos, just like the wogs at Port Said."

This was a day of enormously important decisions for me. In my mind, I listed them: One, I had decided to cease living vicariously through fiction. Two, I would never ever try to drown myself in the surf at Bondi. Three, I had a choice of going back to the Eureka Youth League and meeting Peg again or hanging around and waiting for Ruti—only this time, I would insist on going with her. And finally, I could enter the Vienna Wald for news of Solly.

Decisions one and two, I felt sure, would never have to be faced again. I shuffled the others around, enjoying the luxury of having so many options. It made me feel stronger, grownup; no more Cornwall's Malt Extract for me. Set me a problem and I would solve it, give me a choice and I would like to talk to someone, but, Jacob Kaiser, the responsibility for a decision once taken is all your own.

I pushed open the door of the Vienna Wald. A tinkly bell rang. A voice called out, "So, please to come in. *Komm, Komm,* take a seat."

I moved a few feet inside the door.

"Costs nuzzing to sit!"

The café was long, narrow, and dark. The only light came from tiny table lamps, one to each cubicle. Heavy cigar smoke mingled with the smell of hot chocolate and coffee. It made me queasy. I pulled the door open and gulped in fresh air. The little bell tinkled again.

"So . . . stay, go, stay, go, only please to shut the door."

I slammed the door and marched resolutely down the carpeted aisle. After all, was I not the new Jacob Kaiser who no longer lived in a fictional dreamworld, who rejected death by drowning, who was in love with one girl and had spurned another, and was now ready to take responsibility for his little brother?

"Gott sei Dank, it's only you, Jacob Kaiser. I thought it was the ration-coupon inspector here again." Mitzi Strauss's plump hand folded over mine. She led me to the only vacant cubicle in the café and sat me down.

"Not a word, Jacob, until you've had coffee and cheesecake." She bustled off to the end of the café to where the urns hissed.

Without exception, Mitzi Strauss's clientele were all refugees. Even on this mild Sunday afternoon, they sat in their long coats, their velour hats and battered briefcases on the seat beside them. The tables were strewn with papers; some were writing furiously. Others looked weary and beaten— except for the women, who talked animatedly and puffed on black cigarettes in long holders.

A man across the aisle was staring at me. Finally he got up and came to my table. "You are an Australian?" he asked politely.

"Yeah," I said carelessly.

He took a tin of tobacco from his pocket and opened it. "I would be most obliged, dear sir, if you could instruct me in the method of making from this a cigarette."

I was about to tell him that I did not smoke; I had, on the other hand, spent hours rolling cigarettes for Uncle Siddy

—race horses, he called them, about half the thickness of a tailor-made cigarette to conserve the tobacco. I took the tobacco and papers from the old man, hung the paper from my lip as though I had been doing it all my life, and rolled a smoke. The old man watched every movement.

"Now you have a go, mate." I handed the makings back to him.

"You are a Yid?" he asked me in wonder.

"Well, yes, I'm Jewish, if that's what you mean."

"Das ist wunderbar," he sighed, "you are surely a member of the proletariat." He examined my neatly rolled cigarette. "In Germany I was a Communist at your age, and later I became an official of the Garment Workers' Union. In such a position, I could please nobody. The members elected me because they thought I would get a better deal for them from the Jewish manufacturers. The factory owners said I was a disgrace to our religion—and the Nazis beat up the lot of us." He lit the cigarette and drew the smoke down into his lungs. As he expelled it, he said bitterly, "Solidarity! What a joke!"

Mitzi Strauss appeared out of the half-light of the café. "Now Leon, have you been annoying my young man?" She pointed to the door. "If so, out you go." She set down the coffee and cake in front of me and slid her plump figure into the other side of the table. "Did he tell you he once knew Bertolt Brecht?"

Waves of Mitzi's heavy perfume wafted over me. It permeated the coffee and the cheesecake and even managed to overwhelm the cigar smoke. I leaned back against the booth. She leaned forward, urging me to eat and drink, then she said, "So, let us talk about important things, yes? First, you must know about little Solly. Ach, I have a lot of trouble with him. At school he is always in the fights. That is when

119

he is at school. And my Manfred learns from him." She shook her head in disbelief. "Such a beautiful-looking child to do such things. He steals from my purse—what does he need? I give him—both of them—everything what they want."

As I listened to her, I saw my first summer Sunday, the Sunday of my new resolution, being destroyed. Mitzi Strauss's voice continued to catalogue Solly's and Manfred's misdeeds. Words—*liar, thief, police*—hit me like pellets from a shotgun. I looked past Mitzi's head, down the rows of cubicles where men and women with the troubles of the world on their shoulders tried to rebuild their lives. I felt some sympathy for them, but I did not want to be one of them.

". . . und tomorrow comes the man from the Children's Court to tell me that Solly will be charged with stealing—I can't believe it—they say he stealed, sorry, stole bottles of beer from a delivery truck." Mitzi Strauss slapped the table with her open palm. "Enough is enough already. What do I need such troubles for?"

A feeling of unutterable tiredness came over me. I needed fresh air and sunshine so badly at that moment that I half rose to leave. Mitzi Strauss said sarcastically, "You are just like your Uncle Siddy—when there is trouble, poof, he's disappeared."

"Isn't Uncle Siddy with you, Mrs. Strauss?"

"Well, sometimes he is and sometimes he isn't. Listen, you are not a child anymore. I can tell you, Siddy Kaiser is what you call in Yiddish a *goneff*—a thief who makes jokes while he is robbing you. I am very fond of him. Sometimes he is in my bed and sometimes I don't ask where he is. He gets me the coffee and tea for the Vienna Wald with no questions asked. Enough! What am I—no, what are *we* going to do about Solly?"

The bell over the door rang. Mitzi Strauss got up, telling

me not to go, she'd be back in a moment. I looked up to see Ruti's mother, Irma Kahn, enter the café when I stood up and blocked their way.

"Hullo, Mrs. Kahn, remember me—Jack Kaiser—from the Home?"

"Why, yes, Jacob, of course I do. How are you? And your little brother—Solly, isn't it?"

Mitzi Strauss tried to steer her to a table. Irma Kahn coldly disengaged herself from Mrs. Strauss. "You know, Jacob, you are welcome at our flat, but we never heard from you. Ruti told me she had seen you at the Habonim meeting, and then you went off by yourself. You do know where we live?" She took one of the Vienna Wald cards and wrote on it. "Come soon, Jacob. Ruti would like to talk to you about her studies." She smiled warmly at me and allowed herself to be led to a table.

I sat down again. Mitzi Strauss came back, wagging her finger at me. "So, who's got a girlfriend then, eh? Mr. grown-up Jacob Kaiser? You should always be so lucky, younger man." She looked around the café. "Sit here long enough and half the Jews of Germany and Austria will drink Mitzi Strauss's coffee. But where were we? Ah yes, the police say Solly stole beer from a delivery wagon—not much—what can a small boy carry? But beer, here in Sydney, Jacob, is as scarce as . . . how does Siddy say it? Scarce like hens' teeth!"

In spite of the seriousness of the matter, I laughed.

"It is not so funny," Mitzi corrected me. "Tomorrow he must go before the magistrate. I have called Mrs. Pearlman."

"What was he going to do with the beer?"

I had come as near as I ever would to embarrassing Mitzi Strauss. She patted her forehead with a hankie and hesitated.

"He sells it," she mumbled, "to your Uncle Siddy, and he sells it on the black market."

It was the end of the afternoon. Customers were starting

to leave the café. Mitzi stood up. "I wish I had never met your Uncle Siddy or Solly," she said. "They have brought me nothing but trouble. You will have to be in charge of your brother now, Jacob. I have told this to Mrs. Pearlman. It is finished."

"Are you also finished with Uncle Siddy, Mrs. Strauss?"

She did not answer me.

I waited outside the Vienna Wald until the post office clock struck five. Irma Kahn was one of the last to leave. She was no longer the gaunt figure I had first seen; she was wearing Australian-style clothes and carefully applied makeup. She was saying goodbye to a man who bent over her hand and kissed it in farewell. When he had gone, I spoke to her. It all came out in a rush. I was near to tears as I told her of the trouble with Solly. She nodded knowingly as though it was only to be expected; it was plain she had a poor opinion of Mitzi Strauss. She told me she only went to the Vienna Wald since the death of her husband "because certain things had become necessary." The man I had seen her sitting with, she said defensively, was a former German lawyer who was preparing documents for claims against the Nazis if we won the war.

"Now, Jacob, do not worry, you have two friends—no, you have three."

I looked surprised. "Well, you have Mrs. Pearlman, a very wise woman, then there is myself—ach. I have learned such a lot in a short time—and Ruti is studying to be a social worker. I think she may be your most valuable friend."

We walked together to the tramstop in Elizabeth Street opposite the Great Synagogue. I remembered Ruti kissing me there on the day of my bar mitzvah and Solly using my new handkerchief. Mrs. Kahn was asking me if I would like to come home with her and have tea. Ruti was at the Habonim

122

meeting and would be home later. We sat in the outside compartment of the tram, and I took great pleasure in paying both fares. This simple action seemed to restore my self-esteem. I thanked her and declined her invitation. As I left the tram, she pressed my hand and assured me both she and Ruti would be at the magistrate's court in the morning.

At Bondi, Mrs. Rothfield was waiting for me. "Your uncle is here," she announced with barely disguised distaste. "He offered me some butter without coupons. I do not do such things."

Siddy was sprawled at his ease in her small lounge-room. He waved a hand airily at me. "You're not lookin' too bright, young fella. I reckon y' couldn't go two rounds with a revolvin' door! Tell Uncle Siddy your troubles." He kicked a chair out for me. "Me an' me nephew wants to talk private like, if you don't mind, love."

Mrs. Rothfield, who had in her time faced Arabs, Turks, English, and Australian soldiers without flinching, refused to leave. She sat in a straight-backed chair and reminded Siddy that this was her flat and she would stay right where she was.

"Well"—he turned his back on her and said to me, "by the look on yer face, I reckon you know why I'm here. Young Solly has got himself into a bit o' strife. He has to front up to the beak in the morning. It's only a piddling offense, and nothing serious will happen to him but"—his voice hardened—"I don't want 'im blowin' the gaff on me. We Yids have got to stick together." He gave an exaggerated wink. "Get what I mean, Jack? Like kissin' the *mezuzah*, eh? We're all in the same club!"

Mrs. Rothfield and I looked at each other in disgust and amazement.

I said with rising anger, "A lady I've been talking to says

Solly could be put in the State Home for Boys, and all he's done is nick a few bottles of beer, which you put him up to. They'll say he's in need of care and protection. She reckons that way they can keep him as long as they like." I rushed to Siddy and hit him in the face with my open hand. "I'll bloody well tell them how you keep the Vienna Wald in tea and coffee without coupons, you bloody mongrel. Thank God our father is not here to see what a bastard you turned out to be."

Siddy didn't move from his chair. He rubbed his chin reflectively and said, "You've got a bit o' go in yer, Jack, I'll say that for yer. If anybody else 'd done that to me, I'd 've floored 'em." He got up and pulled his hat down hard on his head in a way that seemed quite threatening. When he reached the door, he said, "I'll be havin' a chat with young Solly. See ya in court."

Mrs. Rothfield slammed the door after him. "You need relatives like that like a hole in the head."

The Children's Court was a few doors up from the shelter where Solly and I had been taken by the police car the day Father died. A gloomy sandstone building in the shadow of the bridge pylon, the only bright part of it was the brass plate outside. Families stood around on the footpath and were shepherded into the court by fussy lawyers and the occasional Salvation Army officer. I had arrived far too early. I saw boys and the occasional truculent girl sitting in the gutter smoking. One boy called out to me as he went through the swinging doors, "What they got you for, Ikey? Pinchin' a leg o' pork, was yer?"

As the mist rolled away from the Quay, I could see the ferries through the gaps in the waterfront buildings. People were streaming off them, oblivious of the misery just a block away. Despite the solid breakfast Mrs. Rothfield had pushed into me, I felt empty and drained. I found a niche in a building where the sun could reach me; a cat rubbed itself against my leg, received no solace, and went on its way. I closed my eyes for a moment. Then I heard a woman's voice complaining about a jammed car door. Mrs. Pearlman had arrived. Solly was wrestling with the door; then they were on the footpath.

Mrs. Pearlman came up to me and kissed me on the cheek. Solly was hanging back by the car. She beckoned to him to join her. I wanted to go to him but was frightened by the intensity that seemed to radiate from him. He presented a terrible contrast; while he was wearing good-quality, stylish clothes, he had the look of a whipped greyhound. His fine fair hair hung lank over his forehead, his face was white and his eyes puffy from crying.

Mrs. Pearlman led me across the few feet that was the chasm that separated us. I put my arms around him; the gesture was futile. Solly's body was stiff and unyielding. I had to prise his hand away from the car door.

"Solly, Solly," I whispered. "Everything will be all right. We're here to help you, Mrs. Pearlman and me. Don't worry."

"Some brother you are, Jack," he gritted. "Pissed off and left me. It's all your fault. We should have stuck together like we said we would when . . ."

I released him and stood back, shattered by the enormity and the accuracy of what he had said. "But . . . but you were the one who wanted to go and live with Mrs. Strauss and that twerp Manfred," I gasped. "It was you who left me."

Mrs. Pearlman cut in. "That will get us nowhere. When all this is over, we shall make other arrangements for the two of you." She linked her arms through ours and led us up the steps of the court. Down the hall, the kid who had called me Ikey was being led away by two policemen. He slid his fingers across his throat as he saw me.

Solly saw the gesture. "Do you know him, Jack?" he said fearfully. I shook my head. Mrs. Pearlman was now talking with a court attendant. The man beckoned us to follow him upstairs into a small, wood-paneled room with benches and a huge Australian Coat of Arms above a raised desk. We sat down on either side of Mrs. Pearlman, whose small stature seemed to me to grow in that impersonal room.

We waited in the gloom. The attendant came and went with bundles of papers. Finally he switched the light on and said in a loud voice, "Be upstanding." A thin, dark-suited man appeared as if by magic from a door behind the high desk. The attendant sat below him. "Call Police Constable Perkins," he boomed out. I looked around, and instead of a policeman, Mrs. Kahn and Ruti came in. Ruti attempted to come to me, but the clerk of the court ordered her to sit down. The constable's squeaky boots echoed around the courtroom. He marched to the witness box and was about to take the oath when the magistrate irritably reminded him that this was a children's court and he need not be quite so formal.

"Well, now," he began, "will Solomon Kaiser please stand up."

Mrs. Pearlman gently prodded Solly, who dragged himself to his feet.

The policeman said in a colorless tone, "My name is Charles Murray Perkins. I am a police constable attached to the Darlinghurst station on the fourth day of October at five o'clock in the afternoon I apprehended the accused—"

"Is he present in court?"

"He is Your Worship that's him with the fair hair—re-

126

moving beer from the back of a brewery wagon the property of Tooth and Company Limited I asked him if it was his property and he said no I then asked him what he was doing and he said—may I refer to my notes Your Worship—"

"He said what?"

The constable flourished his notebook.

"Oh yes, do go on, Constable, and try to remember we are dealing with minors here."

"As Your Worship pleases he said it's for my—and then he shut up Your Worship and never said another word so I took him into custody and we found the address of a Mrs. Mitzi Strauss on him."

The magistrate waved the constable to silence. He consulted his papers, then asked Mrs. Pearlman to approach him. As she rose, I moved down the seat and sat next to Solly. I could feel him trembling. Mrs. Pearlman and the magistrate were talking quietly together. Suddenly Mrs. Pearlman's voiced echoed around the courtroom.

"No! No! You can't do that, he's only a child, for God's sake!"

"Please resume your seat, madam."

"I will not! You cannot do such a dreadful thing."

"Will you assume personal responsibility for him?"

Mrs. Pearlman's spirit seemed to collapse. Her defiant stand disappeared. She said in a low voice, "I am a single woman, Your Worship. What can I do?"

I heard Ruti's voice from the back of the court. "We will care for him, won't we, *Mutti?*"

"Are you a relative?" the magistrate asked.

She shook her head.

"Then I will sign the order. Solomon Kaiser, please stand up. You have already had one brush with the law when apprehended stealing milk. These are difficult times; the country is at war. We cannot have lawbreakers on our own door-step, where people are left without protection from black marketeers, no matter what their age."

He wrote in a large ledger. I held Solly's hand in a fierce grip. His face was gray with strain; I put my mouth close to his ear. "Solly, remember how we made a run for it once before? Away from the coppers and down to the ferries? Listen, we can do it again. You head for the door and go for your life. I'll be right with you. Make for a ferry that's just leaving."

The magistrate was blotting what he had written. He raised his head. "Solomon Kaiser will be detained at the State Home for Boys pending a further review of his case. Call the constable."

"NOW!" I yelled. God, how we ran! We reached the double swinging doors of the courtroom together, swung them open, tore down the passage to the entrance, and leaped from the top step to the bottom. Solly was already a couple of feet ahead of me. As I landed on the footpath, he screamed out, "There's Uncle Siddy!"

Siddy grabbed me as I recovered my balance. He locked an arm around my neck. "Hold hard, Jack, me boy, doin' a flit, was yers?" He held me while two policemen flew past us, after Solly. "What did he tell the coppers? Did he mention my name?"

I bit him savagely on the wrist. His grip relaxed for a moment, and I wriggled free. I took off again, down the hill to the Quay. Far ahead, weaving in and out of the traffic and the crowds, I could still see the broad backs of the police. I could hear whistles blowing and, over their shrillness, the solid blast of ferry horns.

By the time I got to the nearest ferry berth, an eerie silence had descended on that part of Circular Quay. People

128

were hanging over the iron railings. I pushed my way through. I could see a policeman's jacket hanging on one of the spikes. The water was churned up in the wake of a departing ferry, and a life belt bobbed about on the dirty froth. I hung on to the railing in utter fear and exhaustion. Men around me were muttering, "Little bugger chased by the cops . . . tried to jump on the bloody ferry . . . copper dived in after him . . . reckon the kid got sucked under by the propeller . . . ah, y'd think the coppers'd 'ave better things to do with their time instead o' chasin' kids."

I fainted.

10

In the months that followed Solly's death, I was pulled in a hundred different directions. I was unable to make any decisions affecting my life without becoming the recipient of advice from women. They had taken me over; whatever I suggested or showed an inclination for was subject to their close scrutiny and prolonged debate, which, perversely, never coincided with what I wanted. So unanimous were their wishes that they had all the hallmarks of a conspiracy. I never actually saw Mrs. Pearlman, Mrs. Rothfield, Mrs. Kahn, and Ruti in conference, yet their carefully worded recommendations were always preceded by the pronoun *we*. Their wishes were conveyed to me by Mrs. Rothfield. No matter what the topic, she invariably managed to work in a reference to Solly, followed by the traditional Jewish phrase when referring to the dead, "May he rest in peace."

This cliché, meant to comfort those left grieving, had no other message for me than reproach. The women avoided even the slightest hint of my culpability in Solly's death; they achieved this by their very solicitousness for my well-being.

Their intrusion began the day of Solly's funeral, when Mrs. Pearlman, Mrs. Rothfield, Mrs. Kahn, and Ruti all insisted that they should ride with me in the first car behind the hearse. They also agreed to make a common enemy of Mitzi Strauss, whom they forced to ride in the second car with Uncle Siddy. The pathetically small cortege left the dingy funeral parlor in Chippendale for the long drive to Rookwood Cemetery.

Mrs. Pearlman and Mrs. Rothfield sat beside the driver. To my distaste, they chatted away about people they knew, pointed out shops along the way that had Jewish owners, and discussed the progress of the war. As I sat behind them, with the slim figures of Ruti and her mother comforting me, I could see between the two women in the front. I could see the battered old hearse with its blacked-out windows and single Star of David on the rear door. But I could not see Solly and had not seen him since he ran from the court—when we were both so very young.

On that morning, of all the mornings of his short life, I had surely failed Solly. And if it had not been then, would it have inevitably been on another occasion? What if I had drowned myself at Bondi and had never been in the court to whisper to him to run to his death? Should I have fought with Mrs. Pearlman against separating us? Why did I not warn him against Uncle Siddy?

Why did our father have to die and leave me with the responsibility for our lives?

Why, why, why?

It was Irma Kahn's face above me that I had seen first when I came to, that morning at the Quay. My head was in her lap; over her shoulder, I could see Ruti, her face wet with tears. I remember being helped back up the hill and into Mrs. Pearlman's car; Ruti was struggling with the obstinate door handle. I heard Mrs. Pearlman giving orders to her

131

to take me away—"anywhere, just get him away from here."

Uncle Siddy appeared from the fringe of the crowd. "You leave it all to me, missus," he said. "I'll drive and I'll leave yer car in Darlinghurst, right at your office. Don't worry about a thing."

I could see a policeman moving toward us. Siddy leapt into the driving seat. "I'll get you away from them nosy buggers, missus. 'old tight, 'ere we go."

He drove with the same bravado as our father had done in happier days. He tooted the horn and gave exaggerated hand signals. Distressed as I was, I could see that the bastard was enjoying himself. As the car turned out of William Street into Darlinghurst Road, I looked out guiltily as we passed the shabby building where Peg Piper lived.

The car continued at breakneck speed down Oxford Street, through Bondi Junction, and paused momentarily at the top of the rise where I could see the ocean glistening in the morning sun.

"Where to now, miss?" Siddy asked.

Ruti was about to give him directions.

I sat up suddenly and interrupted her. "Drive down to the beach," I ordered him.

"Whaffor?"

"Do as Jacob asks you," Ruti said. He hurled the car down the hill, swung onto the promenade, and halted outside the pavilion.

The beach was deserted except for a fisherman who knew his way through the barbed wire. I got out of the car and walked to the long steps that led onto the sand. I sat down and took off all my clothes except my underpants. A sharp wind whipped the sand against my body. I threaded my way through the vicious coils until I reached the water's edge, then waded through the shallows until the waves could break over my head. I could see the fisherman's line, taut and strung with silver droplets; looking back, I could see the black dot of the car and three figures beside it. One of them was waving. I dived beneath the breakers once more, then came ashore. I stood there for a moment, enjoying the sound of the ratchet of the fisherman's reel, then walked carefully back through the wire to my clothes.

Mrs. Kahn spoke first. "I understand you, Jacob," she said. "You must, how do you say?"

"Cleanse, *Mutti*. Jacob must cleanse himself of what has happened."

"Yes, that is so, Jacob. I understand what you did."

Siddy said, "You mean like the Christians what dunks 'emselves in the river, like?" Nobody bothered to answer him. We got back into the car.

For the first time that day, Siddy's voice showed concern. "As I was sayin', missus, before Jack decided to take a swim, where do youse wanter go? I'm 'ere to 'elp." Ruti gave him directions.

The car swung into a side street and pulled up outside a block of flats. Siddy was out in a flash, wrenching the door open in a mock gesture of courtesy. I saw my teeth marks still fresh on his wrist. "I hope they last forever," I told him. He shrugged and attempted to assist Mrs. Kahn from the car.

She ignored him, waited until the three of us were on the footpath, then said to him with pointed irony, "Do not kill yourself on the way back, Mr. Kaiser."

"No bloody fear, missus," he replied and swung himself into the driving seat.

Mrs. Kahn turned her back on him and led the way upstairs into her flat. From a kitchen cupboard, she took down a bottle of brandy and a delicate wine glass.

"For you, Jacob," she said, then smiled. "Why not for all of us? It has been a terrible experience, and I am sorry to say, worse is to come. I know only too well."

She took down two more glasses and poured a small drop of brandy into each, adding water to hers and Ruti's.

"*L'chaim*—to all of us." She and Ruti sipped theirs, and I gulped mine, enjoying the harshness of the liquor. It coursed through me like fire, burning up the ice in my blood before attacking my head.

"You are used to brandy, Jacob?" She poured me another. Ruti signaled her mother not to give it to me.

I nodded and proffered my glass. I had never drunk brandy in my life, but the pleasure of feeling my senses slip away from me at such a time was wonderful.

"Slowly with this one, Jacob, or you will soon be *shicker!*" I ignored her and swallowed hard on the second glass. Ruti said something angrily in German. She took the glass from me and led me to a bedroom.

"You have had a terrible shock today, Jacob. You need rest more than brandy. You can lie on my bed, and later we shall see what is best to do for you."

I said dreamily, "Is this what you learn at university, Ruti?"

"I am only in my first year, but I am also a girl and I—"

"I may be drunk but I can still tell the difference." I put my arms around her neck as she bent over me.

"I said rest, Jacob, rest and nothing else." She put an eiderdown over me and stood up. I heard the door close as I drifted off.

As the traffic thinned out along the highway, the old hearse seemed to gather speed. I watched in horror as it swayed over the bumps. Ruti saw it too and held my hand tightly. Our driver shook his head.

"We have a new man on," he said apologetically. "Our regular driver is by now in the North African desert, driving a tank."

Mrs. Pearlman murmured something about the war affecting us all and resumed chatting to Mrs. Rothfield, who leaned over the back of the seat and offered me a banana. I took it mechanically and ate it, the soft fruit sticking in my throat.

When next I looked up, the hearse had entered the cemetery and was winding its way along unkempt paths, halting beside a little Gothic building. Our car stopped behind it, and then the car with Mitzi Strauss and Uncle Siddy. A man in overalls came out, consulted a notebook, and pointed to a heap of freshly dug earth a few yards off. He joined another man, and they leaned nonchalantly on their shovels.

We had been more than an hour in the car. Now I wished the journey had gone on forever; I feared leaving its dark and musty interior. Mrs. Kahn and Ruti got out and stood aside for me. Mrs. Pearlman came to the car door.

"You have a duty to perform, Jacob," she said gently. "Our religion says that you must bury your brother." She took a skullcap from her handbag and put it on my head. "When they put your brother in the grave, you must say a prayer and you must help fill it in."

Uncle Siddy came up to her. "Why don't you leave the kid alone, Rosie. I'll do all the necessary."

I looked at him gratefully. Siddy at once became the master of the situation. He ordered the women to stay where they were, supervised the drivers as they removed the small coffin with its black cloth cover from the hearse, and helped them carry it to the graveside. He watched them lower it, calling out softly to them to "watch yer end, mate, not too quick now."

When it was done, he beckoned me over. "We shoulda

had a rabbi here, Jack, but what with one thing an' another . . ." He took a shovel from one of the workmen. "You say a prayer, Jack, if yer know one, and when yer done I'll fill it in—the poor little fella."

I looked across helplessly to the others standing well back, as though the grave held an undefined threat to the living. I was hypnotized by the darting yellow feet of the mynah birds that scratched for worms in the freshly turned earth.

"Please help me," I called out. "What will I say?"

Mrs. Rothfield detached herself from the tight little group. She stood by my side. "Now, Jacob, what does it matter? Praying is something adults do when they cannot think what to say from their own heart. What do you remember best about Solly? You don't have to say it—just think about it."

Suddenly I had a picture of Solly with his head under the tap at the back of the milk cart with the cold white milk streaming all over his upturned face. I started to smile, and the smile became a giggle that turned into a harsh laugh. I could not stop; the sound reverberated around the headstones and came back to me, but by then I was crying, and Mrs. Rothfield was leading me back to Ruti. With my head sunk in her shoulder, I thought I heard clods falling on wood or it could have been the pounding of my heart.

We sat close together all the way home. Mitzi Strauss invited everyone to come to the Vienna Wald for coffee. The offer was refused; Siddy said he needed something stronger. I noticed that as our car passed the little Gothic house, another cortege had arrived. A bearded rabbi led a procession of mourners that seemed to stretch back as far as the entrance gates.

Mrs. Pearlman sniffed. "That'll be old Mr. Schwartz, the kosher butcher. Ninety-three he was, and tougher than the meat he sold."

I must have fallen asleep on the return journey; the sun came through the car window like nourishing food, Ruti's steady breathing was like a murmuring sea that soothed and quieted me. As the car reached Bondi Junction, the women argued over where I was to spend the night. Mrs. Rothfield laid the strongest claim to me.

"A boy—no—a young man needs to be in his own bed in his own pajamas after such a terrible business. Leave him to me."

Ruti blushed at the mention of bed; Mrs. Kahn told Mrs. Rothfield to give me a brandy. "You like brandy, do you not, Jacob?" It was the nearest she had yet come to making a joke.

I was exhausted. I left the car and Ruti without a backward glance. Mrs. Rothfield stood by my bed while I undressed; I was too worn out to be embarrassed, and she knew it. Yet there was one thing more I had to do before I fell asleep. After she left me, I put a sheet of newspaper on the floor, then took my pocketknife and scraped the clay of the cemetery off my shoes. When that was done, I lay down between the cool sheets and thought of nothing.

11

The men at Grayson and Roberts treated me with gruff kindness when I returned to work. It was as if I had been through some manly, cathartic experience; put to the test and emerged if not actually triumphant, at least as a survivor. Their attitude was far more bearable than the cloying affection the women showed me, which only made me want to escape to the lavatory and cry. One of them had pinned a cutting from the newspaper on the lunchroom wall. Solly's death rated two inches on a page mainly devoted to the shooting of a racehorse with a damaged fetlock.

Frank Williams, the printing union representative, no longer addressed me as Ikey; the foreman compositor said I need no longer call him master—Mister Tindale would do, but never to use his first name, which was Archibald, or Arch. I was never sure whether these grudging concessions were due to Solly's death or because I really worked hard at learning the printing trade. The job meant a lot to me; it was the only solid, tangible, real thing in my life. I poured all my waking hours into it, staying back after the working day was done to improve my standards. The machine-room apprentice chipped away at me, telling me, "Whaddya reckon, Ikey, they're gonna take you on as a bloody partner or somethin'?"

138

I finished my first year at the technical college with credit certificates in all subjects. It was the first time in my life I had ever had recognition for any achievement. I told Mrs. Pearlman, who told the president of the Abraham Samuelson Memorial Home, who wrote me a letter attributing my small success to the education and care they had given me and enclosing a postal order for ten shillings.

Mrs. Rothfield said if her English were better she would have written a testimonial letter to Cornwall's Malt Extract, which had assuredly been the reason for my "beating the *goyim.*"

If my world had been full of printers, I might have had a pleasant existence. I could now talk with assurance about typefaces, paper, bookbinding, and ink, and did so—to the seagulls on Bondi Beach. I had grown up enough to be aware of my ignorance of the world around me and yet had developed a snobbishness toward learning, a protective carapace that saw me make half a dozen starts to call around to Ruti's flat and get no further than standing outside on the footpath.

The printery sometimes sent me on errands that took me past the university. From the tram, I could see boys and girls walking up the hill with books and notepads or sitting under the Moreton Bay fig trees in tight discussion groups. I knew Ruti was among them, somewhere, swotting, as they called it. It was impossible to relate that life to the work-stained boys in their overalls who attended the tech college under threat from their employers that if they failed, there were plenty of others glad to take their place.

I also feared that if I once more resumed reading and took refuge in books, I would fall back into a pit of introspection and never get out of it.

In all this, I found in Mrs. Rothfield an unexpected ally.

"You are doing well at your trade, Jacob?" she asked pointedly.

"Yes, but . . ." I replied.

"But what? You don't enjoy?"

"I'm worried."

"That I can see for myself. So tell me."

"Well, take Mrs. Kahn—she's always on at Ruti about learning and how Jews should strive for an education. Isn't what I'm doing learning too?"

"You've been to that Mitzi Strauss's café, haven't you? You've seen all those educated Jews sitting around with their degrees bursting out of their briefcases? *Nu?* What good has it done them, I ask you?" She threw an arm dramatically at the picture on the wall showing her farming in Palestine. "Better if they had got a little dirt under the fingernails!"

"You don't understand, Mrs. Rothfield," I said, bursting with frustration. "I want to be with Ruti, but I'm afraid—"

"What's to be afraid?" She slapped the side of her face. "Afraid she won't think enough of you because you are a boy who works? With his hands? Who keeps himself? Who doesn't get in trouble?" She stopped and apologized for her slip. "*Ach,* you know what I mean, Jacob. Go to her, be proud of what you have achieved. Three credits you got! What does she want of your life?"

I was not convinced. Mrs. Rothfield's rambunctious reasoning only served to widen the gap. Whenever I thought back to the Habonim meeting where I had seen Ruti so at home with that cluster of Jewish students, with Wolfgang solemnly holding forth, I felt more and more isolated. It was enough to blot out all those occasions when Ruti had been so understanding. In my heart, I knew it was not conviction I lacked but courage and a belief in myself.

140

One Friday afternoon, the foreman asked me if I would work on Sunday on a very special job. "You shouldn't mind too much, Jack," he said half-jokingly. "After all, it's not your Sabbath, is it?"

We met outside the printery in the strangely quiet street. He unlocked the door, and we went upstairs to a factory unnaturally still. All that day, we worked side by side, setting type by hand for a beautiful book on early Sydney Cove. By three o'clock, it was done. It had been proofed on a parchment paper, and the historian would come on Monday to inspect it. The foreman gave me a playful push. "Well done, mate," he said. "Now off you go, there's still time for you to meet your girlfriend." He slipped a pound note into my hand.

"No," I said, unable to match his bravado, "I'm too tired. I'm going home."

But once out in the street, I felt like a pup let off the leash. I ran up the street then stopped. Why shouldn't I meet a girlfriend? The Town Hall clock chimed four. About now, the Eureka Youth League would be finishing its meeting and the Habonim starting theirs. Oh, the luxury of having a choice! Peg Piper or Ruti Kahn? A Socialist worker or a Jewish intellectual? With one, I had a common bond of religion; the other had shown me spontaneous, unquestioning acceptance.

If I went to Ruti, would she understand that today I had created something beautiful with my own hands, something I had done almost intuitively, that I was entitled to call myself a craftsman rather than a tradesman? Could I equate this accomplishment with her goal of a higher education?

I had only minutes left to resolve my dilemma. Was I going to be *Chaver* Jacob, a pioneer in Habonim, dedicated to rebuilding the Land of Israel with Ruti at my side or

Comrade Kaiser, working for the revolution with a girl who had lived in the same street as Ben Chifley?

I saw Peg first. Or, rather, she saw me. Her voice rang down the empty street. "Got a deener for the gas meter, Jack?"

Her very boldness put spirit into me. I shouted back at her, oblivious of the absurdity of two kids slanging each other in an empty street on a Sunday afternoon.

"I can do better than that, Peg. I've got a quid to spend."

She walked toward me, high heels ringing on the deserted pavement. "I'll bet the moths have eaten it, Jack."

I took out the pound note and waved it at her. "What's that look like, then, eh? Scotch mist?"

She stopped a few yards off, feet apart, hands on hips, her head thrown back. "Well, well, my little Jewish comrade," she drawled mockingly, "you could have had me for a shilling once and turned me down. Now you want to buy me for a quid!"

I crumpled the note in my hand and stuffed it back in my pocket. Peg watched me, then said sardonically, "Don't you reckon I'm worth it?" She turned to leave. "You're a real ragged trousered philanthropist, aren't you, sport?"

I caught up with her, and we walked side by side down George Street, together but separate. Once, when her swinging skirt brushed against me, it brought back the warmth her words had canceled. Peg kept her head turned away from me as though she were only interested in the shop windows. I looked straight ahead, my eyes fixed on the arch of the bridge. I did not want to lose her, nor did I want her to think that I was angling for an invitation back to her room.

I said, "Ever walked across the Harbor Bridge, Peg?"

"No."

"Like to?"

"With you?"

"Yes." I took a deep breath, flourished the pound note in front of her, and said, "We could have a beaut time at Luna Park with a quid."

Without taking her eyes from the shops, she laughed. "Last of the big spenders, that's my Jack." Then she turned to me. "I reckon you're all right for a four-be-two, as my old man used to say."

Before I could take offense, she added mischievously, "Try to keep a shilling back for the gas meter!"

Peg thrust an arm through mine. I wanted to tell her of Solly's death but was reluctant to spoil the pleasure I imagined might lie ahead. Instead, I talked about the work I had done that day. She took my hand and examined the printing-ink stains approvingly, then showed me how her own hands were cracked from so much washing up at the hospital. It was a small bond between us, not needing political rhetoric to reinforce it.

"I start real nursing next month," she was saying, "with a uniform and a red cape and all. But I'll be going back to Bathurst to do my training and—" She broke off. "You're not listening to me, Jack. I said I'm going back to Bathurst."

I heard her, all right. I tried to steer her across to the outer side of the road. Directly ahead of us, I could see the blue and white uniforms of the Habonim kids gathered in a bunch on the footpath. Even at a distance, I could make out Wolfgang's red hair and the familiar figure of Ruti Kahn in her usual role of rounding up the stragglers.

Peg saw the group too. She resisted my attempt to cross over. "What's going on down there, Jack?" she asked. I didn't answer. "Come on, let's have a look—after all, there's not much happens in Sydney on a Sunday arvo." She let go my arm and ran ahead. Suddenly she stopped, turned around, and called out to me. "Hey Jack, come here. I think they're a bunch of Jewish kids—scouts and guides, sort of, by the look of their uniforms."

There was no turning back. I dragged out each reluctant step of the way with Peg still beckoning me on. When I finally reached her, I was resigned to the inevitable. Wolfgang saw me first. His greeny gray eyes took in Peg, recognized at once that we were together, and greeted me with an ironic wave. Peg said, "Fancy that, the redheaded fella knows you, Jack. Who is he?"

I shrank from telling Peg of all that had gone before; a girl from Bathurst could not possibly understand how a boy from Cologne, Germany, could come to be leading a youth group on a Sunday afternoon in Sydney, New South Wales, Australia.

I mumbled something about Bill being just a bloke I knew. He was pulling the grille of the door back. The kids filed through. Ruti was still rounding them up. Only when the last one had gone in, did Bill go up to Ruti and point to the two of us. My vision of a walk across the bridge, rides at Luna Park, and a sputtering gas fire in a Darlinghurst room dissolved in an instant.

Bill and Ruti came up to us. Peg took off her glasses, patted her hair, and said, "Well, aren't you going to introduce me to your friends, Jack?"

I felt a chill wind on the back of my neck. I was conscious of my ink-stained hands. I could not speak. In that moment, I was aware not merely of the two girls but of the two worlds they represented and the choice confronting me.

Bill said, "You do not look so well, Jack. Perhaps you are having a cold?" He bowed slightly and put out his hand. "My name is Wolfgang Schlesinger, and here is Ruti—"

Ruti interrupted him. "Oh come on, Bill, we can't go on forever with that old German stuff." She laughed and said, "At University, I am called Ruth. Ruth Kahn. Now Jacob, who is your friend?"

Peg chirped up. "Poor old Jack looks as though he's lost a quid and found a tram ticket." She stuck out her hand. "I'm Peg Piper, and I'm a nurse—well, I will be one day, won't I, Jack?"

Somebody called out to Bill from inside the building to come and get the meeting started. He paused a moment to see if Ruti would join him, then went inside. Ruti contrived to isolate me from Peg by asking why I had not been to see her and, she added with hasty propriety, her mother also.

Peg observed the two of us closely. She had put on her glasses and stood with folded arms as though she were about to watch a Ping-Pong game. While I was working out an answer to Ruti's question, Peg said sarcastically, "Do you know him well? Is he always this chatty?"

Ruti said, "Perhaps he talks more with you. He may need a nurse more than a social worker."

The two girls circled around, pretending to inspect me. Peg said, "Mmm, we could both be wrong. Let's ask him."

"Will you two stop it," I yelled. "I don't need a nurse, and if I want a social worker I can call Mrs. Pearlman." I turned to Ruti. "Look, Ruti, I have been very busy at work, and although you may not think so, even apprentices have to study. It's not just for university students." I remembered Mrs. Rothfield's instructions. "And I have just had an exam and got three credits."

"I am very pleased for you, Jacob. Perhaps now it is over, you can come to our meetings."

Peg suddenly became interested again. "Oh yes, is that what those uniforms are for? Is it like the Eureka Youth

League?" Before either Ruti or I could answer, she added, "That's where Jack and me met."

Ruti said, "That is a communist youth movement, is it not?"

"Too right," Peg replied. "Up the bloody workers and all that, lots of marching and singing the 'Internationale.' And we go on weekend camps and swim in the nuddy!" She giggled infectiously. "Is your club, or whatever it is, like that too?"

I told her I had only been once—to either of them. Ruti looked relieved to hear it. She appeared reluctant to explain Habonim to Peg, who then asked her if it was a secret society. Oh no, Ruti said, not at all. She explained it was a youth movement meant to train people to become farmers in Palestine when the war was over.

"Now that sounds more like it," Peg exclaimed. "It beats all that dreary Marxist theory we're supposed to learn." She gave me a playful push. "Are you meeting this afternoon? What about Jack and me joining in too?"

Suddenly Ruti was signaling me with her eyes and an almost imperceptible shake of her head. But Peg's quick intelligence intercepted the message as clearly as the spoken word. Ruti was reminding us that until we had met, Peg and I were on our way—anywhere but to the Habonim meeting.

Peg stood her ground defiantly. She put her glasses on again, folded her arms, and said in a steely voice, "Aren't I good enough for your bloody club? What've you got against me, eh? Is it because I'm a mick or a communist, or maybe you don't like pantry maids or country girls." She pushed me toward Ruti. "Why don't you tell her, Jack—tell her how you were in my bed not so many nights ago and—" She broke off and said, "Oh, don't worry, we were only snuggling up out of the cold."

Ruti moved away from me so that the three of us, whether by accident or design, now seemed to be isolated from one another. In my mind, I was no longer in George Street. I was standing on the craggy promontory of the southern headland of Bondi Beach, where our father had been driven to his death because he was an out-of-work, soft-handed Jew. Below, the waves parted and closed over barnacled rocks that frothed and eddied like the filthy harbor vortex that had swallowed Solly. I shivered at the memory. It would be with me forever, but I would use it to protect myself from a similar fate.

Far off, I could hear Ruti giving a studentlike explanation of the Habonim movement. Words like *heritage* and *history* and *ancient homeland* circled above and about me. Now and again, Peg would throw in a phrase about "equality" and "wanting the same things" and once, raising her voice, demanding to know what they were arguing about—it seemed to her they had more in common than what kept them apart.

I wanted to shout from the cliff tops that I knew what the difference was, that I wanted to be rid of the burden of it, and in reality I did not belong with either of these two girls or the places in society they represented. I knew and loved them both for what they had done for me, but they could do no more. Their very presence had defined my own position. Now at last, I would seek my own identity.

I moved away from the two girls, who had given up arguing and were actually talking about farming. Peg knew how to milk and pick fruit; Ruti was earnestly explaining how social work was not the same as socialism. I leaned against a lamppost. The sound of the two voices made me very happy. After a while, their conversation started to tail off. They shook hands, and Ruti called out to me.

"I've got to go into the meeting now, Jacob. I'm sorry

we've been chatting such a long time, but Peg has invited me to visit her uncle's farm at Bathurst in the holidays." She went to the grille door, looked back once, and slipped inside.

Peg said, "You know that's the first Jewish girl I've ever spoken to? She's really quite nice."

"Well, you'd be the first Irish Catholic communist she's ever met, I'll bet," I said. "And for that matter," I added, "how many Jewish apprentice printers do you know?"

"Only one with a quid in his pocket," she replied cheekily.

"I've got something else in my pocket too, Peg. Something I've never shown you."

I took out the *mezuzah*, now worn and shiny. Fluff from my pocket had filled up the little opening where the Hebrew letter *shin* was written on the parchment. I blew into it to clear it. "Jewish people fasten it to the doorpost of their homes," I told Peg.

"Why?"

"I've forgotten," I said lamely.

Peg said, "You don't have to lie to me, Jack. If it's something like having a crucifix, I'll understand."

"Well, it's nothing really, only some lines from the Old Testament written on a tiny scroll inside the tube. It's all I have left from my father's house."

The Town Hall clock chimed five. Peg said, "It's a bit late for walking over the Bridge, Jack. I reckon we'd better say good-bye. I'll take a tram home. Look me up when you're a famous printer and I'm matron of Sydney Hospital!"

I looked at my ink-stained hands and thought of the beautiful work they had produced this day. Tomorrow I would do even better. I felt very proud.

"Give us a kiss before you go, Peg."

"What, in the middle of George Street?" She looked quickly up and down the footpath, then gave me a peck on the cheek. "That's all you're getting, Ikey." She laughed. "And you've saved yourself a quid!"

I watched her until she disappeared around the corner. It had been a very good Sunday. Here I was, alone in George Street with a *mezuzah* in one pocket and a pound note in the other, and not a care in the world. The sound of the Habonim kids' singing floated down to the street. Well, Luna Park on my own wouldn't be much fun. I pushed open the shuttered door and went up the stairs.

Bill met me at the door. "Ah, Jack, I am so glad you are here. Ruti and I—me—which is correct? It does not matter. We would like your professional advice on a leaflet we wish to have printed."

I liked the sound of that—professional advice. The words were like ink on a paper that certified me as a valuable person, someone worth knowing, now and in the future.

ABOUT THE AUTHOR

Alan Collins was born in Sydney, Australia. He and his wife now live in Melbourne and have three sons.

After working as an apprentice printer and, later, a journalist, Mr. Collins became the editor of a Jewish community newspaper. He now runs a small advertising agency. Mr. Collins is also the author of *Troubles,* a short-story collection for adults. *Jacob's Ladder* is his first novel.